Harmonia

The Sparkling Garden

I0618515

Harmonia

The Sparkling Garden

www.jcperezbooks.com

ISBN 978-0-692-89711-9

Harmonia

The Sparkling Garden

About the Author

JC Perez is a boredom fighting, imagination inspiring introvert, who awkwardly battles her customer service position by day, and mostly battles mom chores and mending boo boo's by night. She has aspired being a writer since she was 10 but never quite knew how to get her stories out there. She has two young boys, who were the biggest inspiration for Harmonia (they approve this message). She loves learning and insects of all weird kinds (mostly moths). JC Perez loves people and things that are unique and supports individualism.

Harmonia

The Sparkling Garden

Introduction

A small, angelic girl, with hair as gold as a goddess, and dimples in her cheeks, reaches up for her mother's hand, while walking along a leaf stricken dirt road. A tall, beautiful white farmhouse, with green shutters looms ahead in the distance. The girl's blond curls bounce and blow in the wind as she gaily trots along, skipping and humming. Bright polka dotted boots, of pink and yellow, splash in puddles and fling mud on her mother's bare leg from under her dress. Her mother turns around and glares scornfully, with a bit of a smirk resting on her lips. The little girl innocently looks up smiling, she knows her mother can't stay mad at her. She's wrapped around her finger and she loves it.

"Really Alex?" Her mother asks rhetorically. "Come along" she motions, with her hand, as she continues her elegant stride. Her mother is the most beautiful woman Alex has ever seen. Her dark blond hair that looks like silk waves all the way down her back. She wears dresses with gorgeous floral print and has a voluptuous body that fills all the right curves. Alex hopes one day to be half as lovely as her mother. She stands there admiring her for a few moments.

The beautiful little girl smiles sheepishly, and starts to run along as a gust of wind circles leaves up in a cyclone around her blowing up her beautiful curls and traipsing off with her sweet pink bow. Alex stops in her tracks and watches the blowing leaves around her as they seem to dance before her eyes. They seem to beckon Alex to play and dance, and just as she is about to succumb, her mother

Harmonia

turns around once again and scoffs playfully, getting Alex's attention and motioning for her to catch up.

"Look mommy, I made the wind," Alex says innocently as she skips to her mother.

"No honey, the clouds make the wind. You, nor I could ever control nature." Her mother rebuts. The little girl, disappointed, grabs her mother's hand and carries on solemnly looking at her feet. Looking back only for a moment as the leaves drift sadly to the ground. Once again having fallen behind, she hurries along to catch up to her mother who is humming a familiar tune and heading for laundry on the line.

That's the last day she saw either of her parents. Caught in a terrible storm, Alex was the only salvageable thing from their house that night. She can remember walking hand in hand with a fireman, away from the house, a slight gust of wind seems to nudge Alex's chin. She crinkles her eyebrows and looks back at the destruction left behind with sadness. A pink bow blows across the yard slowly as if being kicked by a scolded child, and just for a moment Alex imagines the wind as a reprimanded young boy. Alex remembers what her mom had said previously and looks back at the officer holding her hand. *Nobody can control the wind.* Her head bows sadly to her chest and she swears never to believe in fairy tales again.

Harmonia

The Sparkling Garden

Chapter 1

It was a day like any other day, only this day wasn't like any other day at all! It wasn't every day you learn that there are other worlds and other types of beings. But at first, it was a day like any other day.

It began with rain. Buckets and buckets of rain. It had been a rather sleepless night full of thunder and lightning, and again lots of rain. Her tired green eyes bore dark circles that spoke too loud the truth of how weary she was. Her tiny tan hands scrubbed her tired face as she tried to wake herself from the same dream she had been having for months now. She recalls the dream with regret as she lies there listening to the pitter patter outside.

There she is staring at herself in a circular, old, tarnished mirror. Its frame is a dingy silver color that has a floral design in it, once meant to be pretty but now just seems dark and gloomy. It adds to the air of emptiness. Like she is holding her breath, suspended by seconds. Her face is strange and empty looking. It's something unrecognizable, when suddenly it changes completely and black fog swirls in around her as she feels suffocated and can't see anything. She suddenly she bolts upright in bed, sweat pouring from her face, like an Olympic swimmer.

She shakes her dark blonde, wavy hair, which is sticking flat down to her face, trying to shake away the uneasy feeling. She's been having these recurring dreams almost every night for the past few months and it's really starting to get to her. She doesn't recall the moment they first started, all she knows is they have felt a lot worse lately and it is becoming impossible to shake the empty feeling.

She enters the bathroom to wash her face and dress for the day. Looking disdainfully at her board-straight body that bears none

Harmonia

of the curves her mother used to adorn so gracefully. She splashes water on her face and blinks her eyes a few times before looking out the small bathroom window at the rain, which is finally letting up. Now the rainy day is just a dismal day and she can handle that. She rather likes rainy days. They seem to match her loneliness. Like a blanket of comfort that falls heavily on her emotional mind.

Footsteps crushing rock is the only sound on this crisp, rainy, autumn day, as leaves of beautiful orange, red, and browns list silently to the wet ground. The tender pitter patter of small rain drops on leaves fill the air. The morning jog down her long dirt driveway has become early morning routine, regardless of rain or shine. She has a long, winding driveway that runs for 2 miles between trees and woods, with nothing around except a pond nearby. The crisp November Carolina air, lies blissfully about the upcoming winter. A pair of black yoga pants and a soft, pink fleece sweater cling to Alex's athletic body while she bounds joyfully like a gazelle.

She turns the corner and catches some kind of movement out of the corner of her left eye. She stops abruptly and turns her head, but finds nothing. "I must be seeing leaves falling, or a squirrel," she thinks to herself as she starts back into her sprint. Within just a few seconds, she sees something else out of the corner of her eye. She increases her speed. The movement seems to be moving faster too. She's now running full speed, her toes kicking rocks behind her. A large cluster of leaves seems to swirl to her left keeping pace effortlessly with her every step. She looks over and feels like she sees a face in the leaves. All of a sudden, from behind the leaves she sees eyes and a dark swirl. Her feet tangle amongst each other and she hits the pavement hard, knocking the wind out of her. She closes her eyes as the darkness slowly starts to surround her.

Once again, she's staring at that old tarnished mirror. Looking into an abyss of melancholy anguish. The black fog swirling quickly. She feels dazed and empty. Like a zombie looking for the next meal, she unknowingly leans closer to the mirror until she is caught off guard

Harmonia

by the sound of her name as if it's in crescendo. It's repeating and repeating steadily getting louder and more panicked. *Alex. Alex. Alex*!

When she comes back to, there is an older man standing over her repeating her name, with a wrinkled face and a saggy jaw. She scoots up onto her hands and feet still crouched low, and scurries away from the man, trying not to acknowledge the pain in her scratched knee and elbow. She gazes at him intently.

He is wearing an old brown, tethered, trench coat. It looks sun faded and washed out. His hair is a Golden blond color, while his eyes are the deep color of a beautiful ocean. His eyes are inviting and seem to look right into the warm parts of her soul. They seem to twinkle and bring playful memories of childhood on a warm day. They remind her of a relaxing walk on a warm beach with white sands and no one around for miles. The wrinkles around his eyes imply he has laughed a lot in his life. She feels herself begin to relax as her eyes fall down the tattered coat all the way to his shoeless feet, which are wrinkled, dusty, and worn looking.

"I'm Thomas," He says as he offers his hand, jolting her back to reality as she reaches out her hand slowly, but before she can respond Thomas cuts in "Oh don't worry Alex, I know all about you. Sorry I startled you, but it's imperative you come with me right away." He blurts as he pulls her to her feet.

Alex jerks her hand back suddenly wondering why she let herself feel at ease with some shambled stranger walking down a desolate driveway in the middle of nowhere. Has she lost her mind? It's rare to achieve delirious episodes at the age of 25, with no prior signs, but it seems to Alex, this might be the case. She wonders how hard she must have fallen and whether she hit her head.

Then a troubling thought occurs to her, she starts to wonder if this pitiful old man, might be from a home somewhere lost, with relatives looking for him. Maybe he knows her name from the mail in the mailbox, or maybe...she starts to feel a hint of guilt looking into his deep blue eyes. There was something about his eyes that once again distract her. It's almost as if she has known him all her life.

"I'm sorry, Thomas, was it? May I call someone for you?" She asks sympathetically.

Harmonia

The Sparkling Garden

"What? Call someone for me? Why?" Thomas asks. Alex stands there gaping trying to figure out how to explain what she meant.

"No you can't call someone for me!" His voice rising, realizing what she had left for interpretation. "I'm not senile. I know about the dreams, Alex. I know about the mirror. You have to come with me before we're all erased!" He says excitedly.

"I can't come with you sir, you need to leave. And how do you know my name?" Alex speaks more assertively as she is now visibly frightened and she starts to back away from him.

"I'm sorry Miss." Thomas says as he reaches into his jacket pockets.

"Don't be sorr-" Alex starts to say as Thomas blows a handful of dust from his pocket into her face.

She lands softly into Thomas's arms as he swoops up her legs and takes off walking back toward the trees. A swirl of wet leaves starts up his feet and climbs his body, slowly eliminating each body part into a whirl of dust. Lastly, a face remains within the leaves as it winks and blows away, leaving a drop of dew to fall to the ground.

Harmonia

The Sparkling Garden

Chapter 2

Alex wakes with a start, as she sits up quickly, then grabs her head. Her head feels foggy, and it's pounding like a drum. She's trying to grind the sleep out of her eyes so she can see where she is at, but she doesn't recognize anything. Alex thinks her eyes are fuzzy but realizes when she looks down and that she's sitting on what looks like a giant cotton ball. She reaches down and pulls at some of the bedding which dissipates into thin air.

"It's a cloud..." Alex whispers in amazement. She shakes her head. "No. It can't be a cloud. You can't touch clouds. Wake up!" She tells herself as she starts pinching her arm. She winces in pain as she accidentally pinches the scrape she acquired from falling.

A small green character shuffles into the room carrying a covered, silver, tray, and startles her. Closer inspection shows this character has light green leaf petals where feet should be. Its body is an emerald green color tangled vine of sorts. One that you might find attached to a grape vineyard somewhere in the countryside. The creature is wearing a sort of tuxedo fashioned out of purple grapes. Its face, or what you would call a face, is a lighter heart shaped leaf with a somber expression. He seems to make no note of Alex, as if her presence isn't even slightly peculiar.

"Madam," He mutters, in a gruff voice, as he sets the tray on a table made of a golden lightning bolt and glass, removes the silver cover from the tray, and trots out of the room as if marching to some kind of inaudible command.

Harmonia

The Sparkling Garden

Alex begins to question her own sanity, as she sits befuddled, looking at this tray of delicious puff pastries. Her stomach growls in hunger and her mouth almost salivates at the smell of the spread. She has a mild debate between stomach and brain, but in the end hunger and curiosity win. She cautiously reaches out and picks up a red pastry in the shape of a heart, which smells like strawberry, and feels like a crouton. She delicately at first, takes just a small nibble.

It's delicious! Like a freshly picked strawberry with a glaze and honey. She eats each puff more eagerly, each tasting like a different fruit and a different concoction of sugary flavors. She hadn't realized before now, how hungry she was. She takes a sip from the silver chalice sitting next to the puffs and tastes the sweetest nectar she's ever tasted. She imagines the drink was poured from the most beautiful flowers plucked from a magnificent garden. Her headache seems to melt away with every sip of the sugary drink.

Having satisfied her hunger, and extinguished all of the pastries only leaving crumbs, she decides she should investigate this strange room she's appeared in. All of the walls are white and seem to be made out of the same cloud like substance as the bed. There are royal blue posts standing tall on all four corners of the bed that seem to drip from the ceiling to the floor. The air is cool and almost seemingly damp, but has the feeling of a static charge. The room is fairly empty aside from a wardrobe in the corner made from both the lightning bolt like the table, and the same blue substance as the bed.

In the back corner there's a small room off to the side, almost like a bathroom, but the showerhead is a light blue, puffy, cloud that is constantly dripping. A small squeeze of the cloud causes water to pour out more hurriedly. The sink is made from the same cloud-like apparatus that she tests, as she wets her face still trying to wake herself from the dream she believes she is in. She looks into a small tear-shaped mirror made out of water.

"How did I get here?" and "where is here even? How could a place like this even exist? I must have fallen and hit my head" She wonders, grimacing, picturing her body lying on the gravel road as she is dreaming of clouds and eating sweets.

Harmonia

She walks over to the walls, and touches them carefully. They are all made out of clouds as well, that melt and flex into more constantly. Alex makes her way slowly along the wall and stops in front of a massive lightning bolt door. She examines the handle. It's made out of what appears to be a rain drop! She hesitates momentarily to grab it, afraid that it will bust or that it will just disappear entirely, then she considers that might be what she needs to wake up. She takes a breath, and grabs the handle, with her eyes slammed shut. The handle is cold and wet like a slick dew drop on cool fall morning, but it doesn't bust, instead it is hard and cold, like an icicle. She carefully twists the handle, still in awe of the dew drop door knob, and slowly pulls the door open just enough to slip out.

Alex peeks out carefully as she steps out into a massive, golden hallway that is as tall as two houses and as wide as a street. The light blue floor feels like a polished rain drop beneath her bare feet. The gigantic hallway is enormous and long with several large, arched doors, each unique in their own way. Some look like they're made out of bubbles, others trees, and some made out of other objects. Alex slowly wanders down the hallway her gaze listing quickly from door to door until she comes to two giant double doors made out of a similar blue as the bed in the other room, with outlines in the doors that look like various fish. She reaches up and gently tugs at the massive doors with no result, then more firmly tugs on the handle, made out of coral, belonging to the massive door. It swings open, reluctantly making an enormous loud cracking noise that echoes in the enormous hallway. She looks around to make sure she didn't disturb anyone or anything before looking back toward the doorway.

There before her is a giant wall of water, just standing like a wall in the doorway. The water is too cloudy to see anything clearly through, but there are shadows of fish swimming by. Suddenly a large whale of a fish glides past startling Alex as she takes a step backward and gasps. She looks back down the hallway while slowly reaching out to touch the water. Her hand skims the water like touching the surface of a warm pool. She takes a breath, closes her eyes, and slowly and carefully, while still holding the doorway, steps through one toe at a time, until she is fully submerged and completely through the

Harmonia

doorway. She is standing on what feels and looks like an underwater seabed. The sand squishes in between her toes warmly and the kelp brushes her legs. Tiny little fish come nip at her feet, and the water hits her but not like a giant suffocating wave, like a cool refreshing breath, and she lets go of the doorway slowly. She opens her eyes and sees a shadowy figure of a man sitting in a giant throne a few feet from where she is standing. She decides to proceed carefully toward him to get a better look.

"Ah," he exclaims as he quickly joins her "I was beginning to think I'd knocked you out for good!" He chuckles, slightly amused.

She moves into full view of the man and studies him a moment. His skin is taut and smooth. He is a young man relatively in his 20's with hair the color of gold. He's wearing an odd but familiar long brown trench coat.

She then starts to panic for breath and tries to make her way back toward the door.

"It's ok. Breathe." He advises calmly putting his hands on her shoulders to stop her.

She worriedly takes a small weary breath, expecting to inhale water, but realizes she didn't. She takes a bigger gulp of air still looking at the man. He seems so familiar, but strange. Fish of all colors and sizes swim around them.

"Knocked me out for good?" She questions, confused. She's gasping as she starts reclaiming some of the oxygen she has lost.

"Yes, I do apologize, but it's the only way I could get you to come with me!" He retorts.

Alex looks into his ocean blue eyes and exclaims wildly "Thomas?"

"Why, yes of course. Who did you think I was?" he asks curiously.

"But, you were...much older..." Alex trails off wondering if she had perhaps died today and had been unaware. Maybe this is some form of an alternate universe or afterlife that she hadn't learned about.

Harmonia

"Oh, my skin?" Thomas inquires. "I was drying out. That's what happens when I go in there, and I'm away for so long," he states in a matter of fact tone.

"I must be dreaming, or something," Alex mutters, almost to herself, then to Thomas "What did you mean earlier about the mirror and something erasing us?"

"You are worth more than you know, Alex," Thomas pleads, woefully. "You are a great need to us. We need you to save our entire existence, and everything which we have ever known."

Alex burrows her eyebrows together, and just looks at him for a moment not sure what he means. He has a calm voice and a calm sense about him that is almost familiar. And his eyes like the deep ocean are tranquil and soft. Looking into them is like a lullaby hushing her cries of terror, even in her confusion.

"But I don't even know who, o-or what, y-you are or anything about this...this world you claim I must save. I'm plain simple me. I have nothing to do with any kind of heroic gestures. I'm sorry, but you definitely have the wrong person." Alex exclaims excitedly slowly backing away from him as she unknowingly bumps into a manatee. It scurries to swim away from her, looking extremely discarded as she takes two big steps back to Thomas, and mumbles an apology.

"Your highness, I beg you to understand." Thomas Begs. "Please just give me time to explain. Let me show you around. Let me tell you about who you are. Or I mean, who you were."

"Your highness?" She asks rhetorically. Alex looks around the underwater room. "You're not exactly giving me much of a choice, are you Thomas?"

"There are always choices, Alex, but I am highly recommending that you choose to at least give me a chance." Thomas said with a sly smirk, showing a row of perfectly white teeth.

Harmonia

He takes her tiny hand and they begin walking back toward the door she had entered through. Alex holds her breath as they walk through the doorway even though it was as if she had been in her own bubble and the water didn't seem to affect her. They both emerge back into the enormous cathedral like hallway, dry, as if they were never even in water. Alex turn around and looks at the doorway in disbelief and then at the floor, almost doubting herself and whether she made up the entire scenario in her head, patting her dry hair and dry clothes all the while.

"The different areas don't intermix in Harmonia." Thomas explains nonchalantly as he continues walking.

"Different areas? Harmonia?" Alex asks in amazement, as she trots to catch up.

"There isn't just an Earth like the one you've lived, Alex. There are several different realms here in Harmonia. This hallway, with all the doorways, is called Harmonia" He gestures out toward the enormous hallway.

Harmonia

The Sparkling Garden

Chapter 3

Alex looks around more intently and a little more out of curiosity now, realizing that there are harps and cherubs carved into the golden walls. The ceiling is a beautiful blue that looks like diamonds sparkling in the sun, which is also shining through the ceiling and almost seems to follow them as they move. Each door adorns a different theme, but all are made from a light oak wood. The entire hallway resembles the most beautiful summer's day. And now that she's not completely frightened, she can smell the beautiful scent of a warm summer picnic with freshly cut grass and a slight breeze. "How did she walk through here earlier and never notice the beauty?" she thinks to herself. She smiles softly, as she sniffs the air and gazes gleefully. Each intricate detail is brought to light with each glance, as if magically carved before her eyes. She can't decide where to place her eyes. There are so many beautiful things to admire in each carving as they pass. It's amazing what our eyes are blind to when we are too scared to look.

"How many...realms...are there?" she asks thoughtfully. She wonders what other places could Harmonia possibly hold, and wonders if any of them are half as creative as this massive hallway, and a room made out of an ocean. She starts imagining realms filled with cotton candy and stuffed animals and anything her childhood brain would have accepted.

Harmonia

"There are many more realms than this hallway holds," Thomas says almost as if reading her thoughts "but, in this hallway, there are 6 including mine. My realm is the underwater realm. I keep watch on anything having to do with oceans, streams, lakes, and even frozen areas. I not only regulate all of the water in the Earth realm, but in other realms as well. That is how I knew it was time to come and get you. Almost every realm holds water in some type, and I can only travel through water for long periods of time. As evident earlier, I start drying out once I'm out of water and away from Harmonia. It had been raining a lot on your Earth realm when I traveled," he pauses and catches an overwhelmed expression on Alex's face, and decides to change the subject. "Let me introduce you to a few beings," he says motioning down the hallway.

They walk down the hallway back toward the room that she first woke up in, but about 3 doors down, they stop. She looks at this door intensely. The handle is made of a large, exotic, red flower, and the door itself seems to be entwined with vines and thorns, that move to ravel and unwind within itself right before her eyes. It twists and writhes like intestines trying to process a recently eaten hamburger. Alex feels like she can hear it growling, but it's beautiful and enchanting at the same time.

Alex looks back up to see the creature that had brought her pastries earlier marching down the hall briskly toward them, along with something that resembles a bell with vines for legs and leaves for feet, stalking sulkily further back. The bell of the creature is the color of silver, and has tinsel like strings hanging from the top of bell that resembles hair. It has a long face, with very big eyes, which adorn the longest eyelashes that Alex has ever witnessed. Its limbs are long and lanky and it seems to slink as it walks, with a bashful, awkward stride.

Limping beside the bell and the grapes, a very tall character that looks like something just crawled out of a scary movie. A tall,

Harmonia

gray, skeleton looking figure with rags of almost rotting flesh that appears to dangle from his bones. A partially hinged jaw rests at an odd angle making the skull appear longer than it is. Empty eye sockets appear hollow and black, so she can't tell if the thing can even see her. Alex becomes frightened at seeing the grotesque skeleton and moves slightly closer to Thomas, shivering softly behind his arm. He looks down at her, slightly confused at first, then gives an assuring wink to say that he understood why she was afraid, but that she has nothing to fear.

"Alex, I believe you have already met Seb." Thomas introduces the green leaf man that brought Alex the Pastries. Pointing to the bell looking thing he continues "this is Juneth," lastly pointing to the ghastly skeleton "and this guy here, is named Frank."

Frank rushes to shake Alex's hand, tripping over his bowed feet, stumbling the whole way but, but somehow staying upright until his hand connects to Alex's. Juneth curtsies, daintily, and Seb makes a curt nod, then instantly regains his statuesque stance.

"I'm so pleased to finally make your acquaintance your majesty," says Frank in a rather high pitched voice for such a frightening character, shaking Alex's hand so hard she is afraid it might detach from her wrist. His cold, hard phalanges squeeze into Alex's soft, fleshy hand. He's smiling his eerie boney smile from, what would be an ear cavity, to the other. She's surprised to say, the least, at this gruesome character's friendly behavior. She can't help but be amused at his over-zealous attitude.

"I'm...equally as...umm...happy...to meet you...." Alex stammers out confused, as Thomas puts his hand on Frank's and stops him from shaking Alex's any further. "But I'm not a majesty, I'm just a person." She quickly clears up humbly.

Harmonia

The Sparkling Garden

"Eh, we're umm showing Alex around, and getting her reacquainted with, ummm, Harmonia," Thomas stammers off quickly.

"Alex?" Seb asks, while slyly glancing over at Thomas. A smirk dances briefly across Seb's face.

"We're still working on that as well, Seb" Thomas deflects quickly. Alex gives a questioning look to Thomas, but he doesn't acknowledge her, instead he continues toward Seb. "I am showing Alex around Harmonia, we are going to talk about the urgency of her being here, and why we have come to get her. All will reveal itself in due time, Seb, be patient." To Alex Thomas says "Are you ready to continue our tour?"

"As ready as I'll ever be," Alex replies somewhat withdrawn. She gives a little wave to the strange characters that she has just met. She wonders if she'll ever begin to understand what is going on in this place, but part of her feels better having met Seb, Frank, and Juneth. Although, part of her feels more confused from it.

As they take off walking, Alex looks up to Thomas and asks "What did Seb mean when he said my name like that?"

"Alex is short for Alexandra in your world, but you were once known as Alastriona here. It is a noble name meaning 'defender of mankind.' They are not used to a nickname such as, Alex, for such a great being," Thomas answers honestly. "And before you say it again, you were born for great things, Alex."

"I don't understand what I could possibly contribute, or what I could possibly do to help this place. I'm not magical, or brave, or even that smart. I don't contribute to anything in a big way and about the only thing I've ever truly mastered, was making buttered toast, and even that's a flop depending on the day. I really think you have the wrong person. I'm sorry," Alex digresses anxiously.

Harmonia

The Sparkling Garden

Thomas nods knowingly, as they stop at the door that has giant flowers and decorative birds around the frame. He turns the knob, shaped like a leaf and thrusts open the large door, which makes a loud bellow. They step inside to a garden unlike any that Alex has ever seen. She looks at some of the most amazing looking flowers of all sorts of colors that you wouldn't believe. With spirals, and polka dots, and crazy swirls of color combinations more vibrant than a Dr Seuss book. Wisps of white, feathery, floral delight seem to hang in the air. The sun is bright, and she shields her eyes for just a moment. There are birds singing almost in harmony and there are butterflies dancing in the air all around. The sweet smell of honeysuckle and lilac waft in the air and penetrate Alex's nostrils, making her inhale deeply thinking of a fresh spring day, as a dragonfly almost lands on her nose, then takes off buzzing by.

In the near distance, she sees the most inviting waterfall that she has ever seen. It reminds her of a fantastic oasis that is dropping diamonds, as the mist sprays back up into the air. She gazes around at some of the bounding hills of green and beautiful, orange sun, when her gaze falls upon a dull gray area further in the distance. It resembles graphite lingering in the air, like the shavings from a pencil with one too many mistakes.

It is so far in the distance, yet it still gives Alex a melancholy shiver. She feels cold and alone looking over there. Almost as if it were the exact representation of what empty inside really feels like. She imagines the garden being suspended in time. Hanging in an almost dead empty balance that won't resolve, almost like an unfinished purgatory caught in an absence of thought. She wonders how it got that way. Especially when everything around it seems so beautiful and majestic and paradise. She feels sadness for this beauty, that is being destroyed, and she is shocked to feel the warm liquid indication of a tear rolling off her cheek. She reaches up and tries to

Harmonia

flick it away as quick as possible before Thomas notices she is crying, but it is too late.

"I too, feel a significant wave of remorse when I look into the void," he tells Alex solemnly wiping a rogue tear out of the corner of his eye. "This void is what is destroying all of Harmonia. It is spreading throughout each of the realms, like a plague. The void just undoes everything and leaves emptiness dripping sulkily throughout the worlds and we can't understand why. It started like a small tear in the sky, and has now spread to more realms, increasing in size every day," as Thomas is speaking Alex notices that his face is starting to age slightly becoming more worn and wrinkled.

"How can I fix this?" Alex asks "I don't know how to make things reappear after becoming obsolete," she stresses, creasing the lines between her eyebrows.

"You are the only known Realm Walker. The only being capable of moving between all of the realms in Harmonia. You are the only one who can withstand each realm's natural energy," Thomas pleads "there is no one else who can help us."

"Well when you put it like that, it really relieves the pressure," she says sarcastically bringing a little bit of a smirk to Thomas's face.

"I know it seems like a huge journey, and it is. I also know that learning all of this about the realms and then being asked to save every new being you didn't even know existed seems overwhelming, but we need you, ALEX. We need you to try, because without you, that is our future," Thomas begs, gesturing out to the void in a voice so passionately that Alex feel goose bumps.

He slowly turns and makes his way back toward the door from which they first entered, leaving Alex to stand there just staring at the beauty and she wonders how her world went from a typical human, to a monumental leap into the unknown with leaf people and cloud

Harmonia

cities. She looks back over her shoulder, into the void once more and feels sorrow, as she turns and follows Thomas out of the door and back into the hallway. She wonders, how she can be the only person to fix something like this. How can all of this be real? She doesn't even know where to possibly start. She ponders these questions, as she follows Thomas up the giant hallway.

"I know there are a lot of questions. We've planned a small banquet in your honor while we discuss more about the journey, and then you can decide," Thomas suggests, as he leads her down the hall toward a door that encumbers carvings that represent food and celebration such as meats, vegetables, and a cornucopia. His skin is returning to its original taut, youthful skin that it was in the water room.

As they wander slowly into the dining room, Alex is amazed by a giant table that looks like an enormous graham cracker sitting on humongous turkey legs. She stops and gazes around the heavy room, which seems to be made of honey ham and different sliced meats. The aroma smells like a Thanksgiving family feast. On the graham cracker table, lay some of the most exotic looking fruits and possibly vegetables that Alex has ever seen. They have polka dots and hoops around them, and they are all made of strange bright colors and shapes. There are some that appear to be oozing a cool whip type substance, while others appear to be coated with some kind of glaze. There are giant fuzzy round things, and some shaped like asterisks.

Already seated in front of waffle looking bowls are Seb, Juneth and Frank. Seb is sitting very firmly with his back straight and nose in an upward angle. Juneth blushes bashfully and waves over her shoulder while the bell part of her becomes a fire engine red color. Frank sits there drooling hungrily and staring at the food, mouth agape. Thomas walks over and takes his seat at the head of the table while saying hello to the others.

Harmonia

Upon Alex's entrance to the table, Frank looks over at her with a big goofy half jawed smile, as Juneth reaches over and starts trying to hinge his jaw back on one side. After having been seated, they all begin digging in and passing food, like a family that hadn't seen each other for years, reconnecting and talking over food. Seb speaks of tasks that need to be fulfilled by Thomas, and Juneth bashfully, and excited tells Thomas of her excitement with a grasshopper. They are all talking over each other at once, happily and friendly. Except Frank, who just engulfed a whole turkey leg in one bite, which extended his whole skeletal body a good 3 inches as it passes along his bony figure and falls to the floor with a plop.

Alex, unsure of what is what, is very weary of which foods are meats, or vegetables, or fruits, and takes small amounts of just a few items sniffing them gently before placing them in her bowl. She glances at each of the other 4 to see them all enjoying everything they've placed for themselves, and she decides to give these foods chance. She is pleasantly surprised to enjoy each item differently. Even though this one spoonful is as green as a frog, and the consistency of pudding, it has an amazing robust flavor that reminds her of chili. She picks up an oblong purple thing that has the white, cool whip oozing out of it. Surprisingly, it tastes like shrimp Alfredo. She enjoys all of the food so much, she reaches for seconds while the Juneth and Thomas smile warmly.

"There is a book that can give us insight to what is going on with the void in some of the realms, but the only problem with that is...well, no one has ever seen this book," Thomas finally offers seeing that everyone is starting to finish their plates.

"Then, how do you know if the book even exists?" inquires Alex, in between bites.

"The Tree of Wisdom told us about the book once," Thomas responds

Harmonia

The Sparkling Garden

"How does a tree know that the book exists, but you have never seen the book? Can trees walk here in Harmonia?" Alex asks wondrously, wide eyed.

Thomas chuckles a little as his eyes sparkle and Juneth and Frank burst with laughter at the thought of walking trees. "No, of course the Tree of Wisdom can't walk. The book was made from some of the branches. That's why we know the book can tell us how to stop the void," says Thomas dabbing his mouth with a napkin.

"So, how would I find this book?" asks Alex, now feeling a bit foolish.

"The book was last seen by the Tree of Wisdom, maybe it can tell you how to find the book," Seb offers.

"The Tree of Wisdom is in the Sparkling Garden," says Juneth in a voice so small and sweet. Juneth's eyes look bright and cheerful. "I like the Sparkling Garden," she adds shrinking back down into her chair with a soft smile.

"It sounds beautiful, but where is that?" replies Alex, still wondering why a walking tree is funny, but a talking tree is fully expected.

"It's one of the realms here in Harmonia. I will take you to the Sparkling Garden door first thing in the morning," promises Thomas "but first, you should get some rest. Getting to the Tree of Wisdom can be quite tiring."

"Oh, I feel like I have lost all track of time here, or what the concept of time really is." says Alex "It doesn't even seem late?" she says in a questioning way.

"Time, well, the way you know it to be, is very different here in Harmonia. We do not live by the same standards such as day and night," replies Seb. "Shall I show you to your chambers?"

Harmonia

The Sparkling Garden

  She finishes chewing the remainder of food, and follows Seb to the door. She waves goodnight to everyone as she thanks them for the good food and hospitality. They begin walking toward the cloud room she originally awoke in. She enters, and closes the door behind her.

Harmonia

The Sparkling Garden

Chapter 4

Alex is sweating profusely, white faced and staring into that same old tarnished mirror. Her eyes look completely black. The aroma of rusted metal and smoke linger in the stagnant air all around, like the horrific aftermath of a building fire that was just recently put out. Alex thinks to herself, if depression had a smell, this would be it. Her reflection continues to stare back at her blankly. Even though she is frightened to the bones, she cannot look away. Those black eyes have her mesmerized, when suddenly her jaw slowly starts to drop into a silent scream. Black fog exhales from jaws and spirals outward, slowly encompassing everything around her. She wakes up choking and gagging, unable to breathe.

It takes her several moments to finally catch her breath. She looks around, confused about where she is. The white puffy room reminds her of all that has happened, and the reality that this isn't a dream sets in really hard. She starts crying to herself in disbelief of all of the confusion her life has become over the last day. It's so hard to differentiate between her nightmares and reality lately, and she feels like she's absolutely losing her mind. Seb busts in the door carrying a tray of food and a small pouch. She quickly starts rubbing her eyes and tries to hide the fact that she was crying, as he sets the tray and pouch on the stand beside her.

"When you are ready to go, meet us in the hallway." Seb says statically as he marches out the door.

Harmonia

The Sparkling Garden

Alex looks at the tray which has similar looking pastries as she had earlier tasted, but her stomach is still in knots from the dream, so she only nibbles at a few of them. She opens the green sack and finds a small knife, a small spool of string, and a medium size flask. She grabs a napkin and wraps a few of the pastries in it, and tucks it into the pouch as well. Alex carefully pours some of the juice into the flask, spilling it only a couple of times, and twists the lid tight before also placing that in the pouch.

She gets up and walks into the bathroom and cleans her face with icy cold water. She then pulls her hair back with her hands into a hair tie, and looking into the mirror she takes a huge breath and shakes her shoulders. Lastly she throws the strap of the pouch over her shoulder and heads to the door. Hesitating at the door she looks back into the room, knowing she is about to embark on a life changing journey. She grabs the handle and slowly emerges out of the room. Seb, Thomas, and the others are congregated close to a big door, waiting for her in the enormous hallway.

"Hopefully you had a good sleep," starts Thomas, as Alex walks up to the group. "Getting to the Tree of Wisdom can be a treacherous journey so we've given you a few items to help you along the way. They aren't much, but it's the most useful items we could find around Harmonia. Juneth is also going to accompany you, since she is the only being from the Sparkling Garden, and she knows the way."

Juneth blushes bashfully and flashes a bright orange color. "I've only been there a few times, but I definitely remember the way," she assures twisting sheepishly back and forth.

"I'm happy to have you as my traveling companion," replies Alex. "Shall we get going then?"

Harmonia

They move to the door that Alex had been entertained by previously. The door is made of flowers and moving vines that twist and move. Its thorns twist and almost thirst to prick. The entry way beckons for someone to enter and explore, almost like a taunting call from an older sibling into known danger. It's intriguing and unsettling, screaming danger while still showing off its beauty. They stand there hesitating to open the door, both in trepidation for the upcoming journey. Alex carefully grabs the handle and twists, opening the strange new realm they are about to enter.

"Don't separate from each other, and don't trust the pixies," calls Thomas as they enter the realm.

There, in front of Alex and Juneth, stands flowers at least seven foot tall. The stalk is as big around as Alex and fuzzy like a caterpillar. It waves to a gentle breeze back and forth like a swaying pine tree. Up in the sky at the top of the stalk is a large pink flower. Next to it is a large blue flower and further on there is a rainbow array of colors that create a forest of flowers, making it impossible to see too far ahead. Like a rainbow canopy the cluster shields most light from the sun, yet still they perspire under the warmth.

They begin navigating between the stalks. Alex reaches up and carefully pushes one of the giant leaves up out of her path, pollen dropping on her like fairy dust, causing her to sneeze repeatedly several times. They look back and can't see anything through the green stalks and rainbow petals, except more flowers. The ground is soft brown soil that squishes as they step. Both silently moving along until they finally come upon a clearing ahead where the blossoms seem to dissipate, and more of the sun starts to shine overhead.

"So this is where you are from?" Asks Alex, trying to make light conversation.

"I live here," answers Juneth "in the flowers."

Harmonia

"You live in the flowers?" asks Alex, almost to herself. "Don't they wilt after a while?"

"Nothing goes bad here in Sparkling Garden!" Says Juneth with a slight chuckle then she becomes solemn, "well except in the void."

And with that both of them fall silent again. Each reflecting on how the void affects both of them separately and together. They find their way to a small parting within the massive flowers and come out onto a gently rolling hill top. The grass is emerald green on top of this hill and it glitters brightly in the sunlight. From the hilltop they can see several more glimmering hills and shimmering brightness. The refraction of light is almost blinding so that Alex has to shield her eyes with her hands. In the distance she can see massive gray and white mountains looming. There are several dirt paths in the grass, but only one path goes all the way through to the mountains and seem to run in between. The mountains are tall and intimidating, with a layer of fog hovering over them.

"Let me guess, we're going to follow that path?" Alex asks as she points toward the mountains

"Have you been here before?" Asks Juneth surprised at Alex.

"No, I just assumed, since that was the scariest looking path that we would have to go that way." Alex says smirking.

"Not all things that look scary are actually scary," says Juneth hesitantly. "Like Frank for example, he is downright frightening at first glance, but he's really very sweet, and silly, and kind." She turns around so that Alex can't tell she's blushing, but her whole bell turns bright red.

"That is very true," Alex agrees "Are you and Frank...ummm..?" Alex prods lightly, trying not to overstep or offend.

Harmonia

The Sparkling Garden

"Oh...No...No, no I just...I mean he's really nice, but....I'm a...well, flower, and he's a...I don't know..." stammers Juneth turning a deep shade of purple now.

"Oh, I didn't mean to assume. You don't have to be embarrassed, I was just curious," Alex quickly tries to recover reaching out and touching Juneth on the bell lightly.

Juneth falls down in the grass and looks up at Alex with tears in her eyes. "Well, I do really like Frank. I always have, but I'm way too shy to tell him," she confesses desperately, twirling a blade of grass around one of her viney leaf fingers.

"It's ok to be shy. That's part of what makes you who you are. You should tell him though, because he deserves to know that such a great plant thinks that he's great too. I mean what's the worst that could happen if you tell him how you feel right?" Alex insists. "Although," she adds, "I'm not exactly the best person to give advice on relationships. I've never actually been in one. But I do know that you seem like a really nice...um flower, and you should just tell him how you feel."

"Really? You think I should?" Asks Juneth turning to look at Alex, her big droopy eyes heavy with tear drops.

"Of course! You never know what could happen until you try, but if you don't try then you know nothing ever will," Alex assures sweetly, making a mental note to tell herself that next time she's indecisive. "Now back to the task at hand, which path do we follow?"

Juneth and Alex start down the long dirt path that leads between the Mountains both talking and Juneth promising to tell Frank as soon as they return. At the entrance to the trench the air around them suddenly changes to a dark mystic kind of air, as both the girls stop their chitter chatter. Alex crosses her arms and shivers a little while looking around hesitantly. Back on the hills you could see

Harmonia

bug type creatures, butterflies, and birds swooping and flying. Here in the trench, it's just eerily quiet with no living organism in sight. The dirt even changes from a brown color to a dull gray color, resembling smushed gravel. Both Alex and Juneth are stepping as carefully and quietly as possible, but it seems like every rock makes a huge crunch, which echoes throughout the entire canyon like a loud cannon blast.

Out of nowhere, the ground begins to grumble and shake. Little pebbles are bouncing along the dirt, and rocks start falling from above their heads. The ground is growling, like a low rumble of a giant's hungry stomach. Juneth and Alex reach for each other while looking around for a way to escape. Bigger rocks start falling from the mountains. The girls are reaching everywhere to try to steady their footing, unsuccessfully, when Alex leans slightly onto a boulder. The boulder shifts to reveal a small entryway for a cavern. Alex taps Juneth and points to go in. They both shimmy into the small opening right as a huge rock busts outside closing the entry behind them.

Inside the cavern, things are calm and surprisingly quiet with the drip, drop sound of water falling from stalactites to cavern floor. The cave is a luminescent blue and peculiarly bright to be the inside of a mountain. The smell of the air is sweet and warm. Alex makes her way over to the dripping pool of electric blue water and delicately caresses it with her fingertips. It's sticky like syrup. So she slowly brings some of the substance to her lips and carefully smells it, then she tastes the goo. It tastes like cotton candy. Like an oozing drip of candy gook. Juneth is bent down at the small pool, already drinking some of the sugary drink. They stake a glance at each other with a sigh of relief and share a short chortle before heaving another sigh and continuing on their feet.

They turn around looking in different corners of the cavern for a way out. Each checking different walls and behind stalagmites for any kind of exit.

Harmonia

"So, can you still find your way from here?" Alex asks Juneth.

"As soon as we find our way out of this cave, I should be able to," replies Juneth looking around. She points to a small opening in the ceiling of the cave that is letting a small pool of light shimmer through.

"It looks like that's going to be our only escape," relents Alex, very unhappy with the height. She isn't scared of the climb, it's the fall that scares her, but being trapped in a cave forever scares her more and she's already feeling claustrophobic.

They slowly start climbing some of the soft blue glittery rocks toward freedom. They pull themselves higher onto each porous boulder until they find one that is flat. The next rock above Juneth's head is a little taller than her or Alex can reach on her own. Alex tries to jump and grab onto the ledge but a small piece crumbles in her hand, sending her plunging back down. Juneth reaches out and steadies Alex so she doesn't fall off of the flat rock and they both look at each other in terror as she teeters a moment before finding her balance once more.

Finally, they manage their bearings and are able to stand on the ledge. Juneth offers her petal for Alex to step up on and Alex hoists herself onto the ledge, belly first, as her arms quiver. She spins around and slides down low enough to grasp one of Juneth's vines, which snakes around Alex's arm and she assists her onto the ledge. Both lean back on the ledge in relief and just look up in trepidation of the next few rocks to climb before they reach the top, not daring to look down.

Taking a moment to catch their breath before moving on, Alex takes the pastries from her bag and offers one to Juneth. She refuses but looks insatiably hungry. Alex eats her pastry and they both simultaneously stand up and continue climbing and helping each

Harmonia

other, ledge after ledge. They work together and finally make it to the opening. Alex squeezes through first to emerge on top of a mountain ledge looking down on a huge stream, more sparkling trees, and flowers everywhere. There are a couple deer down by the stream and some birds flitter by on their way to join the deer. Alex reaches down to pull Juneth up and they stand, staring down the mountain at all the beauty that lay before them.

"Wow! That is a beautiful sight. This is why I love the Sparkling Gardens," Juneth exclaims, as she smiles widely.

"So, how do we get down?" Asks Alex, ruining the moment of the perfect view with her reality check.

Juneth's smile fades to a confused smirk. "I thought you would figure that part out," she muses.

Alex looks around bemused, trying to figure out exactly how they are going to get down from the side of the mountain. Alex looks over at Juneth, who is looking around everywhere frantically trying to figure out what to do. Then, Alex sees it. Right above Juneth's head, a thick, sparkling, green vine dangles from the ledge and seems to glisten its assistance to helping them down the mountain.

"That could work," points Alex. Juneth nods in agreement and they start inching their way close enough to extend a fingertips' grasp. Juneth reaches with all of her leafy might. Finally, she is able to wrap her own viney tips around the trailing plant. She gives it a light tug, but it's hung on something. She tugs a little harder and finally it breaks loose, sending a few rocks to topple over their heads. She pulls the vine until it stops and won't budge anymore, then she starts climbing down slowly. When she puts her feet firmly on the ground, she looks up at Alex, who follows suit.

Alex starts her descent slowly climbing down as careful as can be, but as soon as Alex gets right above Juneth's head, the vine snaps

Harmonia

and she falls, crashing to the ground with a loud thud. The fall knocks the wind out of her at first, then, after catching her breath, she starts laughing hysterically. Juneth joins in too.

Alex gets a shiver up her spine that stops her laughing abruptly. Her eyes dart all around, scanning the water, the trees, and everything within sight. It's that feeling that someone is watching her. It's that eyes on her feeling that is making her blush, and driving a chill up the back of her neck, as she tries to figure out who, or what? Juneth is still enjoying her chuckle, not noticing that Alex has stopped. Alex shakes her head and smiles back at Juneth trying to shake the uneasiness, when out of the corner of her eye she notices movement over toward the river. She's startled by what she sees and just sits there gaping and rubbing her eyes.

A tall white horse with a single glistening silver horn and a long red mane made of dancing fire is standing there staring intently at Alex. They lock gazes and Alex is almost hypnotized by the unicorn's deep red eyes. She is so captivated, it's like she can't even move, and time itself seems to stand still. All around, nothing moves, everything is still. The gallant horse walks with slow intent straight toward Alex and Juneth. Juneth is still, with her head down, frozen in time. Alex can only watch as the tall fiery unicorn walks past her and slowly picks up its trot until it quickly just blinks out of sight like it was never there. Juneth resumes her chatter and giggling like nothing ever happened and all else around them seems to carry on.

"Did you not see that?!?" Asks Alex wildly as she interrupts Juneth in mid laugh. At first Juneth isn't sure what just happened. Her face whips backward, caught off guard, like someone being struck with whiplash.

"See what?" She asks concerned.

Harmonia

The Sparkling Garden

"Th-the unicorn!!" exclaims Alex throwing her hands up excitedly.

"Nobody has ever seen a unicorn," Juneth explains shaking her head "There used to be a story about unicorns being able to manipulate time or something, but that was just a story."

"I know what I saw. It was huge and had a fiery mane." Alex begs, trying to describe it. "Big fiery mane and red eyes!!!"

"Maybe the Tree of Wisdom will know?" offers Juneth, shrugging, thinking maybe Alex is just tired or stressed. Maybe she hit her head when she fell from the vine, and knocked herself out just long enough to hallucinate.

Alex tucks her chin down to her chest feeling defeated. She knows what she saw was real, well, as real as anything else she has seen so far. Although, with that logic, how could she believe anything she knew, or knows now? What if she's just a crazy person?

They continue to walk down by the river that seems to sparkle the most amazing assortment of rainbow colors, under the crisp blue top layer of refreshing water. The ground is green like a shimmering meadow. The sky is an electric blue color and the bugs seem to be made of diamonds, rubies, and emeralds. They buzz around and *tink* when they land on the giant flowers nearby. Looking further ahead, the girls see an enormous forest that looks dark and looming. These trees have roots that stick up and twist and turn like the evil turmoil of a magician's spell weaving around. The air is dark like a shadow looming to catch any light that dare to shine.

"We have to go through the whispering forest." Juneth says in a hushed tone as she points toward the nightmarish jungle.

"I figured as much," replies Alex with a large gulp.

Harmonia

"The forest can be tricky and sticky, watch your footing, and try to remain as quiet as possible." Juneth advises as they approach the edge.

On the edge of the forest now, the trees seem much taller and girthier. They seem to forbid entrance into the darkness. The leaves seem to rustle as they approach, almost offended that they dare to challenge entryway. Feeling much more scared than she had originally, Alex draws a big breath, and puffs out her chest, letting her breath escape slowly and noisily out from between her lips. She tucks back a rogue hair from her eyes and proceeds forward into the forest, climbing one of the tall roots and ducking under the next.

"I guess now is as good of a time, as any," she says disappearing into the darkness.

Harmonia

The Sparkling Garden

Chapter 5

The first steps into the trees feel like a heavy blow to the chest. Anguish sets in like an elephant on her chest. The silence is so loud it's deafening. Alex feels like she can hear her heartbeat in her ears like a loud parade, muffling any sound of birds, or crickets you would typically hear in a forest. They tip-toe around leaves and sticks trying excruciatingly hard not to make a sound. Juneth carefully and slowly leads the way, meticulously planning every step cautiously, like a performer walking on hot lava stones. They pick each step with baited breath, waiting for the crackling or popping of some twigs to cause a horrendous fatal end.

Ahead lies a massive white haze. Alex blinks trying to figure out what it is. As they come closer, she realizes this is a giant spider web. Alex stops, like she just hit an invisible wall. She looks at this web that seems so thick, she can't even see through it. She starts looking around possibly for another way around the web. The webs are all over the place. In every corner. She panics! Juneth turns and notices Alex standing, shaking. She carefully makes her way back to her.

"Alex, we have to go through here," Juneth urges quietly, while gently tugging Alex.

"I can't," affirms Alex standing her ground.

Harmonia

"Alex, we have to keep moving," insists Juneth now a little firmly.

"I. Just. Can't," proclaims Alex looking at Juneth pleadingly.

Suddenly the web starts shaking in front of them. Bouncing up and down like an excited child on a trampoline.

"You have to come with me now, or it's going to come after us, now come on Alex, we have to go now!" Juneth pulls Alex's arm. Alex starts to refuse again.

Just then a large, thin, fuzzy leg drops down through part of the web just over to their right shoulders. Juneth grabs Alex by the hand and ushers her to be quiet with a shhh with her finger to her lips. They slowly climb left through part of the web, going in between particles and trying not to touch any strings. Refusing to even breathe, they move carefully, like two interpretive dancers, they tango in between strands of web, inching their way further from the arachnid's foot.

A quick movement stops them in their tracks as they stoop low to the ground and watch the web bounce above their heads. With eyelids clamped as tight as the Jaws of Life, Alex slowly begins to open her eyes and turn her gaze to the large spider sitting almost practically on top of them. She expects to see giant kaleidoscope eyes and a huge black fuzzy arachnid, but what she sees is much worse.

The torso of the thing resembles a human torso but it's twisted and distorted. It has an upside-down face on a human head, with black hair that is stringy with greasy sweat dripping from the long tangled locks. The head rotates slowly to the side where Alex can make out multiple eyes and a lopsided, elongated jaw, with a mouth full of pointed, sharp, jagged teeth. The eyes are black and empty. There is no nose at all. The legs are long and fuzzy like that of a spider, stretching out to thin points, but bent backward from the way they're

Harmonia

supposed to look. The smell is pungent and sickening like that of decaying animals.

Alex looks back into the empty eyes, and feels the same empty, alone feeling that she felt when Thomas showed her the void back in Harmonia. That seemed to be forever ago. Its eyes seem to be swirling with a black fog like the one from her nightmares. The mouth of the thing salivates and drips the pungent death smelling ooze toward Alex's face. She turns her head quickly and softly gasps as it falls onto the back of her head leaving a pile of warm liquid to slither down her head. Her hand rushes up to her mouth to hide a gag.

Quickly, the things head jerks, eyes down toward the web where Juneth and Alex crouch. Its mouth opens wide and it makes a loud, inhuman screech, bellowing toward them as the web starts shaking from all angles. Juneth grabs Alex's hand and they take off running full dash swatting away from the sticky web as they try, unsuccessfully, to dodge most of the strands. Alex slows down for a moment to peel off some of the sticky web that has adhered to her clothing. A quick rustling sound, like a child romping in the leaves, echoes behind them, encouraging them to run faster. The hairs on Alex's neck prick and goose bumps run up her arm as she can feel one of the things catching up, the rancid smell on her neck. She barrels her head down like a torpedo and pounds the moist ground harder than she ever imagined she could run. Like an Olympic runner they duck and slide until the web starts becoming more spacious until there is suddenly none.

Panting and gasping vehemently Alex and Juneth collapse behind a large tree, once they are sure they are safe. They can hear the evil screeches from the things echoing behind them in the distance. Winded and trying to catch what little oxygen seems to be in this humid forest, they gasp for each breath loudly with sticky, sweet, sweat running down their faces. Alex's face is red and glowing like a

Harmonia

cherub, as she wipes some of the sweat out of her hair. Juneth's bell is pale blue.

"What were those things?" Alex pants out slowly between gasps.

"Chasms," replies Juneth gapingly. "They came after the void appeared."

"The void changed a lot of things like that?" Alex asks, hands on her knees as she sits up to look at Juneth.

"Some. I guess I didn't realize what all had changed since I've been in Harmonia, I think things have been getting worse." Juneth replies sadly "I've only read about Chasms until now. They are supposed to be things of evil wickedness. You can definitely tell by looking at them. I remember how much the stories used to scare me, they are nothing compared to the real thing." Juneth adds while catching her breath. She seems to pale just talking about them.

Harmonia

The Sparkling Garden

Chapter 6

Alex pulls the flask of juice out of her bag and takes a large gulp, then hands it over to Juneth, who studies it like a foreign object. She sniffs at it then pokes at it with her viney hands. She takes a small taste then spits it out.

"THIS is NOT plant food!" she yells, disgustedly, pushing the flask back into Alex's hand. Her bell becomes a fire engine red color.

Alex jumps back for a minute and tries to figure out how to take Juneth. She's never heard her yell, or get upset. She starts twisting her hands around and fumbling with the flask lid and she looks down.

"I just thought, that I would offer, well you see, running makes me thirsty..." Alex trails off innocently, barely making eye contact.

Juneth looks ashamed, while turning back to silver, then explains "Certain things are toxic for a bell like me to ingest. I thought you were handing me plant food, or water like we had in the cave, what is this stuff?"

"It's some kind of juice I got from Harmonia," Alex claims. "I would never try to hurt you. I'm not even sure what kind of juice this is," she admits still ringing her hands.

"That's ok," says Juneth, relenting. "I just had a bad experience when I was younger. Somehow my water bottle got filled

Harmonia

with the river water, which is bad for flowers, and I drank it, and the Tree of Wisdom and Thomas had to regrow me," Juneth explains putting a hand on Alex's shoulder.

"Oh, well let's not let that happen again. So, do you never die?" Alex asks curiously starting to feel a little better.

"Of course I do," answers Juneth. "I can just be regrown, as long as it's soon after my petals fall apart exposing my core."

"So how many times have you been regrown?" asks Alex?

"Only once." replies Juneth. "It's very painful, because you can feel the decaying and then the regrowth of your new body."

Alex rises to her feet, and then helps Juneth up.

"Ok guide, what shenanigans shall we face next?" She jests playfully.

"Ha-ha, hopefully no more Chasms. Those things really freak me out." Juneth replies honestly, while looking around for the right path.

Walking through the forest quietly so as not to alert any other beings, or not beings, like the Chasms, the girls start to hear a loud pounding sound. Almost a roaring sound.

"I smell water," Alex acknowledges, sniffing the air like a hunting dog.

"We're almost to the waterfall," Juneth replies happily.

The trees start to look bigger and more spaced out. More and more trees have vines of green and orange and low lying branches of yellow and blue. The floor becomes more like sand but looks purple. The leaves all sparkle like emeralds and diamonds. Alex is admiring the leaves shining and glimmering, looking up and all around when, BAM! She walks right into one of the low lying branches.

Harmonia

The Sparkling Garden

"You'll have to pay better attention than that," Juneth says while trying to stifle a giggle.

"Obviously," Alex says while rubbing the side of her head with her hand and ducking under the limb. She looks back at the branch in anger as if it made her hit her head, then looks forward and notices Juneth has gotten ahead of her a little.

Suddenly, a small, cute little girl in a pink dress, no bigger than the size of a dime lands on Alex's hand. She turns her hand around to get a better look. She's a tiny girl with purple wings and jet black hair. Her little skirt is made of some kind of pink fluffy dust that puffs as she walks. She waves with her tiny little hand and Alex smiles from ear to ear. The tiny little thing starts doing a little shuffle and bats her eyelashes while flipping the end of her long ponytail off of her shoulder. She starts to curtsey and bow. Alex is beyond amused, almost as if she is in a trance, just watching the thing. She is amazed at how tiny and cute the thing is and starts to wonder what it could possibly be?

Alex notices the cute little things eyes. What is wrong with those eyes? It's almost as if they're completely whited out. All of the sudden the cute thing smiles showing tiny, pointy, sharp teeth. Rows and rows of teeth. Alex stops smiling and looks a little frightened, and with that, the pink dress thing takes a huge bite out of Alex's hand.

"Ouch!" Screams Alex, as she flicks the cute thing off her hand and into the tree. "What in the world was that?" She looks down at her hand which is starting to bleed, but is the blood purple?

"What was what?" Juneth asks as she rushes back over to look at Alex's bleeding hand.

Alex falls slowly to the ground, trees spinning and the sound of Juneth's voice slowly fading out. She peacefully closes her eyes and as if she just blinks, she sits back up. Alex looks all around at the

Harmonia

falling leaves and bare trees that gather around. She knows this gravel driveway all too well. The smell of rain and the pale gray color of rocks surround her.

Confused, she pushes herself back to her feet and looks around at the familiar driveway that leads to her own house. She whirls around in every direction, assuming she must have hit her head really hard and just awoken from a terribly detailed dream. "How long have I been out?" she wonders aloud, as she looks at her hand, which is now not bleeding and roughly scabbed.

As Alex begins a slow trot down the road, she notices an eerie stillness, a deafening silence and she stops in her tracks and looks around, taking in her surroundings. Everything looks so familiar yet very strange and threatening. Everything looks like it is supposed to, but her heart starts beating harder as if she's in danger. "I must still be jumpy from my dream," she says, trying to convince herself that everything is ok.

Suddenly, Alex's eyes fall on an old tree off in the woods. It's hollow and black; dismal and gray. Nothing significant looking about the large, bare tree, but the ominous feeling that she feels in her gut when she looks at this tree seems familiar and foreboding, almost sinister. The hairs on the back of her neck begin to prick as she slowly starts her trot again, resistant to take her eyes off of the tree. Just as she turns away and gets into a full sprint, she stops again a few feet away. She looks to her left and sees the exact same tree only this one on her opposite side and slightly closer, this time the holes resemble a shadowed face almost like a rotting jack-o-lantern.

"I must really be losing my mind," she thinks aloud. "To be scared of a tree. All trees look alike. They're trees," she exclaims loudly, as if convincing a large audience. She even throws her hands up extra theatrically to prove a point. *"But they don't feel like this one."* She thinks to herself.

Harmonia

Alex shakes her head at her own dismay and once again begins her ascent back to her house, where she can be away from talking plants, fish people, and evil chasms. She is determined to make it to her bed so she can sleep off these weird hallucinations or whatever is going on in her head, and she has made up her mind that she will not be distracted again. She's obviously stressed or fevered, she thinks. Abruptly she slows in the middle of her sprint again noticing that tree very obviously on the side of the road just ahead angled to her right.

"That definitely has never been there before!" she gasps out loud shaking her head and furrowing her eyebrows.

She turns over the thoughts in her head. She feels like a cornered dog. She's not sure if she should run past as fast as she can, or if she should turn around and head the other way, but how can she be stalked by a tree? She wonders. She stops while trying to pursue any kind of logical explanation for these strange happenings. Slight movement to her right where the tree is seated accelerates her decision, and her heart rate.

She decides to run through the woods directly around the tree in a direct path for her house. She takes off running full speed directly through the woods. A branch snags her shirt. Another one snags her yoga pants, which draws a little blood. She keeps running, darting between limbs and trees. Fleeing as in hot pursuit she can see her house through the tree line when out of nowhere, there comes a black fog so thick she can't see anything. She slows down but keeps moving closer, trying to push her way through the dense darkness. The forest becomes exceedingly dark and so hard to see through she has to physically squint, and almost wonders if she could navigate better with her eyes closed. Alex tries to gather her bearings and force her way closer to home but now she's not even sure which direction she's going. She feels lost and disconnected from reality; from everything. Her breathing slows down, and her chest tightens.

Harmonia

The Sparkling Garden

She feels like the darkness is seeping inside of her. For a moment she thinks to herself that this will be her final moments, and she's suddenly angry.

"I will not die here, and I will not die now!" She shouts in her mind. She starts pressing on, walking and trying to push the black fog out of the way. It feels heavy and thick like oozing oil from a transmission system that hasn't been changed in a while. She opens her mouth to catch her breath and she tastes rotten egg and rancid meat. The fog is like death swirling around in a cloud. Faintly, Alex notices an eerie light in the distance. She shoves toward that light with all of her might, not one worry what that light might be. The light becomes slightly brighter and brighter the further she pushes. Out of nowhere, it seems, gallops the fiery looking unicorn that she had seen earlier down by the water with Juneth. For a moment she's happy to see it, then she realizes it's charging straight for her!

Like a ton of bricks slammed into her face, she falls and keeps falling the darkness swirling above her but she doesn't hit the ground. Instead, she just keeps falling, forever it seems. Her face is numb from the impact and she feels her body going limp. So many thoughts going through her mind, like a scribbled old road map, but you can't decide where you need to be. She fades slowly into softening slumber.

Visions of strange things that seem familiar, yet not at all, flash through her head. Visions of real things she's done or been through but with a slight twist. An image of her walking with her head down up her driveway and a shadow lurking slowly behind her. Slinking slowly from tree to tree, or rock to rock, it seems to stalk her. Another image from a birthday party she had as a child. All the other children are playing and having fun and Alex is sitting to herself talking to a flower. The flower in this memory, isn't just a regular flower, it has Juneth's face. A thought of that day with her mother floats by and the pink ribbon dancing in the wind. Her strange uncle, who resembles

Harmonia

The Sparkling Garden

Thomas, whispering in her ear about a power to discover. What could he mean?

Harmonia

The Sparkling Garden

Chapter 7

Her eyes snap open to see Juneth leaning over Alex, with worried look and a pale yellow color bell. She notices Alex open her eyes and she squeals with excitement as she hugs Alex closely to her. Alex gasps and looks around frantically. She coughs feeling fresh air in her lungs. Momentarily she is baffled by her surroundings. It's dark but there is ambient lighting. Twilight at dusk plays funny tricks on the eyes. Shadows cascade like an afterthought bearing down on your conscious. Alex is frightened by the shadows and by all the images she just saw, but they are slowly fading from memory fast.

"What happened?" Alex trembles, feeling cold and scared pulling her knees to her chest and hugging her knees. Unable to recall anything except for the darkness she just endured. She feels like it was long ago that she had even seen Juneth's face. How could so much happen in such a short time.

"Stupid pixies," Blissfully replies Juneth as she turns around and starts fiddling with some grass and making big gestures, "those things are tricky. At first they're all nice and cute and entertaining. You never would guess they hold so much venom in one little bite. I'm just so glad you're back. I was afraid it wouldn't be enough."

"Pixies? What do you mean that it wouldn't be enough? How long have I been out?" Alex inquires almost too afraid of the answers.

Harmonia

"You have been out for 2 whole days. Don't you remember getting bitten by the pixie?" Juneth asks putting her leafy hand on Alex's shoulder.

Like a distant memory that happened long, long ago Alex starts to have the faintest incline of the incident with the pixie. And running from the chasms. Her memory feels foggy though, like nothing was, or is real. She looks at Juneth, concerned. She is an empty stalk with no leaves except where her hands would be, and her bell, which is really pale.

"Oh Juneth, what have you done?" Alex asks incredulously, gasping and putting her hand to her mouth.

"I couldn't let you die," Juneth answers sheepishly. "You are most important!"

"I'm no more important than you are!" Alex exclaims sadly.

"Really, it was no big deal," Juneth lies, "It'll grow back in no time. Enough blabber, let's get on with our mission," Juneth stands trying to hurry the change of subject.

"Wait!" blurts Alex, "When I was, wherever I was, the void, err, I think it was the void, was all around me. Attacking my home and it almost captured me until the unicorn charged into me knocking me out. What was that? It didn't feel like just a dream." Alex starts rubbing her forehead still feeling the pain from getting knocked in the head.

Juneth looks at her with a scrutinizing look. "I told you, nobody has ever seen a real unicorn. But there used to be stories about them," she starts, hesitating at first, but Alex looks so intrigued. "It was said that the unicorns all took on different elements long before beings were formed. The elements interacted harmoniously playing and laughing amongst themselves."

Harmonia

The Sparkling Garden

"This made the universe angry and jealous because he was alone, so he created beings of all different types, with greed and anger, and other afflictions to cause turmoil between the unicorns." she continues "At first the unicorns tried to live among the beings, and show them their peacefully accepting ways, but the beings were brash and would not listen to understand. The beings began killing unicorns to harvest their elements, causing war amongst themselves. Supposedly, what was left of the unicorns, divided themselves and the beings to limit some of the fighting and squabbling, creating Harmonia as we know it now as the safe place away from hate. Story says, that one day the rainbow walker would come along and save the entire universe and bring back the unicorns, but that's just a story. If there were any unicorns, someone would have seen them by now. I mean, other than you." She shrugs. "And I've been with you both times you've claimed to have seen them. Besides, the rainbow walker is supposed to have a power beyond belief. Anyway, it's all just bedtime stories for kids."

"It just feels so real. I know what I saw," Alex relents. After a moment thinking to herself she asks "Anyway, what is next on our list for travels?"

"Well, we should be almost there." Juneth says excitedly. "It's getting dark, we'll wait until light before heading out again. We're safe here for another night." Juneth is worried that Alex has hit her head or something and doesn't think it's safe for her to travel in her condition.

Alex can't stop thinking of the story Juneth told that night as she's trying to go to sleep. She tosses and turns but finds very little rest. Head spinning with visions of this fiery unicorn she's seen twice already. How did it all fit together? How did any of this fit at all? Of course she didn't see herself as anything special, but twice she had seen this same unicorn. Why was the universe jealous? And what, or

Harmonia

who, exactly is the universe? She nods off into a restless slumber, chasing a fiery unicorn down a sparkling hill laughing and playing. She is about to catch up to it when she starts to fall and the sky turns dark and she is abruptly awaken with a jolt.

It's still dark, but there seems to be light coming up in the sky. She gets up and walks around a bit. Alex props herself beside a large fungi, looking off into what would be the sunrise on earth, but it's just a broad light here creeping up steadily at all angles. Each small detail about what lies ahead starts to become clearer as she sits quietly admiring the sight. She wishes she could be sipping a coffee and eating donuts. She reaches in her bag and pulls out one of the pastries. It's hard and stale, so she tosses it over the hill. She becomes disappointed when she notices the flask is empty as well so she takes a deep breath and just looks over the horizon.

She can see a forest of over-sized mushrooms below the hill, ahead on their journey. They tower above 6 feet tall and some are wide, some are just skinny. They adorn different many different colors. She can see them leaning all different ways. Mushrooms, as far as the eye can see climbing a hill in the distance. Her eyes catch something just past the mushrooms out on a ledge. It looks like a giant weeping willow tree. Just as Alex is about to wonder to herself if that is the Tree of Wisdom, Juneth walks up and breaks the silence.

"Isn't she elegant there in the distance, sitting on that ledge? I've always thought this was the most beautiful place to enjoy her splendor, although, being quite honest, this is the furthest I've ever come by myself." Juneth admires with a look of content on her face.

"What are we going to run into in there?" Alex asks as she points toward the mushrooms. Juneth looks like Alex pulled her from a trance.

Harmonia

The Sparkling Garden

"Those should be relatively safe. Don't touch the ooze though, it'll make things all wiggly." Juneth advises. And with that, they take off walking toward the mushrooms with a new determination.

Harmonia

The Sparkling Garden

Chapter 8

The smell of fungus and earth hits them like a double edged sword. The stalks on the mushrooms are as big around as an old oak tree. Most are white, some are oddly colored. The caps of the mushrooms glisten of blue, green, red, and purples. Condensation drips from the caps in a creepy melodic dissonance, as they hit the stalks and shorter caps. The air is moist and cool beneath the mushroom forest, a fresh relief from the already hot sky. As they make their way around every vulva, they tread carefully, trying not to touch anything. They pass a snail, as big as Alex, slinking slowly across the mycelium floor, leaving behind it a glittering trail of slime that glitters in the daylight. Its terminal knobs of the gastropod, flick over to look at Alex and Juneth as it quietly inches away. Studying them as if they are intruders into his personal home. Then he quickly flicks them back to front position and keeps moving along.

About midway through the mushrooms they happen upon a, somewhat of a giant insect city, where large ants are crawling one way, bus-like caterpillars of blue and purple are carrying pill bugs of green and greys, and giant grasshoppers are stepping overhead. Juneth and Alex carefully trek their way across the bug traffic, only perhaps interfering with one lone pill bug, as big as a shopping cart, who looks up at them in dismay for having to stop just a second, and then he scurries to catch his place in line back where he was, squeaking all the while.

Harmonia

Alex is watching this little scurrying bug so intently that she isn't watching where she is walking and turns around and squishes right into a humongous, slimy, slug. Thick, green slime oozes from her face and her hair as she turns up her nose and tries to sling the slime toward the ground. It splats against the ground and it drips from her body. The slug tries to scurry off, looking as if he has just been violated in the most horrific way.

"I think I'm going to be sick," Alex says as her face pales and she heaves. Juneth, giggling quietly, finds Alex a large piece of mushroom to use like a towel and dry most of the ooze from her face. She thanks Juneth and they begin walking again, making sure to pay attention to their surroundings. Getting further away from the buggy chaos, the air gets cooler and quieter, sending an eerie chill up Alex's spine. It won't be long until they reach the Tree of Wisdom, and it's been such a long journey already, how can this just be the beginning?

As she was so deep in concentration, Alex never even noticed a slight humming sound until the giant hornet makes its first assault, luckily hitting a mushroom instead of Alex or Juneth. They both look up to see a swarm of hornets buzzing around above the mushrooms. But these hornets don't look like anything Alex has ever seen. These are gray and black in color and seem to be made of fumes, with black spikes poking out from their bodies. They buzz around in circular motions, and they seem to aim directly for Alex.

"These must be from the void!" Juneth screams, as she dodges another attempt from the hornets.

"How?" asks Alex, jumping under a mushroom cap that breaks when the hornet flies into the corner and she runs under another mushroom.

"I have no idea," says Juneth. "C'mon," she yells leading Alex through the mushrooms. Juneth ducks and dodges the bees leading

Harmonia

Alex to a large hollow log lying in the grass just past the mushroom forest.

"We have to get rid of these, but I'm not sure how!" Juneth cries, trying to block the hollow end of the log with a large mushroom cap.

"I wish it would rain, I bet that would run these bees off!" Shouts Alex, as she sits there almost angry with the sky for not opening up and dumping buckets of rain. The girls peek out around the mushroom cap.

Like a perfectly timed theatrical event, the skies open up and down pours the biggest rain drops Alex has ever seen. She looks at Juneth, her mouth agape. The bees begin to be pelted by enormous drops of rain that extinguishes their existence the moment the rain touches them. Each one of bees slowly blinks out of the sky, one by one, and the rain slowly dissipates back to a partly cloudy day.

"What was that?" asks Juneth looking at Alex in disbelief, dropping the mushroom cap and exiting the log slowly.

"I don't know but it was weird right?" asks Alex walking out to join her "I was just saying..."

"You made the rain!" accuses Juneth turning around suddenly and pointing at Alex, with a humongous grin on her face.

"You can't make rain," says Alex with a smirk remembering what her mother said a long time ago. Her mind reels back to how she really believed she could influence the wind, and how children can believe in everything before anyone tells them it's wrong.

"You just did," argues Juneth dropping her smile in disbelief.

Harmonia

The Sparkling Garden

"C'mon," Alex urges walking toward a giant ravine of winding jumbled vines. Juneth gives in and follows along still repeating over and over about how Alex made the rain.

The deep ravine contains vines that must only exist in this strange garden. Alex stands now at the edge of them. Looking up, she can see the Tree of Wisdom sitting high upon the ledge, just past the vines. She sits looking bright and mysterious. Her low lying branches hide the trunk creating an enigmatic appeal.

The vines seem to move and creep, writhing like snakes or worms. They have sharp green thorns that seem to ache for blood. The vines themselves whisper beckoning's, that can't quite be translated, but you know they mean to put you at ease and urge you to touch them. Their leaves hunter green and a deep red seem to beckon for just one small prick.

There are enchanting looking flowers that seem to blossom straight out of the thick of the vines. Bright colored flowers that scream innocence where there should be alarms. An unsuspecting butterfly lands on one of the astonishing flowers to drink its sweet nectar. The flower's petals become razor sharp, and animated, like a tree chipper looking for the next large oak. The butterfly struggles to fight its way off of the flower, while it is pull down in between every speedy petal until it is completely gone. It happens within seconds even though it feels like she's watching in slow motion. Alex turns in disgust and sees Juneth reaching for one of the flowers right at that moment.

"Juneth, Don't touch that!" Alex alerts raising an arm to Juneth. The razors start swirling just as Alex pulls Juneth's leaf hand away.

"Wow! Thanks." Juneth says, tucking her hands behind her back, quickly.

Harmonia

As the sweet smell of nectar rises up to meet their faces, they both begin into the ravine. Alex pulls out her small knife from her bag, and uses it to cut small vines from their path, and every once in a while, cut a threatening flower. The girls move slowly and carefully between the vines, careful not to alarm it. Feeling like a mouse in a snake pit, they move almost in sync with each other, making their movements as lucid as possible. Each step carefully calculated.

Sweat drips from Alex's forehead. Being under all of these thick vines they start to feel claustrophobic and weave their way faster through the vines. Alex can hear the whispers growing louder, taunting and calling. They are driving her crazy. She starts humming, but the whispers are getting louder, so she hums louder. Juneth seems bothered by it too as she has her hands up to her face and her bell has changed to a mixture of colors representing a terrible tie dye t-shirt. After what seems the longest time, they emerge on the other side of the ravine, just below the Tree of Wisdom. The vines seem to hiss in disappointment behind them, trying to coddle them back through.

The girls sigh in relief as they climb the embankment to reach the ledge where a tree that resembles an oversized weeping willow sits. Branches dangle low and swing all the way to the ground. The leaves are yellow, like an electric cage encompassing all of the knowledge. They shoot sparks out around them like a busy bug zapper. Alex makes the mistake of reaching out to touch one of these branches, which kindly sends out little shocks that feel like a static charge. She quickly decides not to touch the branch and pulls her hand back to her body. The girls crawl their way under the main branches, beneath a small gap at the bottom, to an opening with a bulbous round tree trunk. They realize the trunk itself is almost 6 foot wide as they circle the base, in awe of its splendor.

Harmonia

"So. How does this work? Does it have a face? Or talk to us?" Alex asks slightly intrigued but mostly just genuinely curious. She nudges the tree but tries to be careful not to poke what may be a face.

"I. ummm. Well, to be honest, I'm not entirely sure," Juneth says bashfully and turning a pale red. They look at each other for a few moments and then at the ground thoughtfully.

"Oh mighty tree, please bestow upon us, this book upon which we seek!" Alex yells out loud while gesturing with a low bow in front of the tree trunk.

They wait a moment looking around in all directions, then at each other. Nothing happens.

"Well, that was my only genius thought on how to find the book," Alex says in a glum way. "Have any suggestions?" She asks Juneth, once again perky.

"You're not going to like it, but....maybe if the book was made from the branches, then the branches have all of the wisdom?" Suggests Juneth struggling to keep a positive tone.

"The branches that electrocute you when you touch them?" Alex asks sarcastically while pointing to one of the pulsing limbs which sends a small electric charge to her fingertip that she pulls back quickly after the shock.

Juneth shrugs her shoulders as if to say, "What else are you going to try?"

Alex lets out an unpleasant grunt of disapproval and playfully stomps her feet while asking, "And which branch do you suggest I start with?"

Juneth shrugs again. "Beats me. Maybe one of the oldest looking branches?"

Harmonia

"Yeah, but which ones look old?" Alex asks walking around gazing at all of the different limbs and leaves. "Screw it." She says as she reaches out and grabs one of the branches close to the trunk. A sharp buzz and a zap and she lets go of yelling, "Ouch!"

"Any wiser yet?" Juneth asks trying to restrain a giggle.

"I know better than to keep yanking on these things. Now what?" Alex asks as she leans against the enormous tree trunk.

At that moment, a door opens in the trunk exposing a staircase going down in the center of the tree, almost causing Alex to topple over.

"Ha! Guess I am wiser!" Alex jests as she carefully places one foot at a time on the narrow winding steps that lead into the darkness. The smell of old wood rises to greet them. The inside of the tree is very quiet.

After going down at least five feet of stairs the darkness is so thick that neither can see anything aside from a small dim light several feet below them. Alex starts fumbling for her bag around her hip and starts blindly digging. Juneth runs into her then backs up a few steps.

"What are you looking for?" Asks Juneth quietly.

"I have some matches." Alex says still rummaging through her bag in the dark, finding a few more stale pastries that she tosses carelessly out onto the steps.

"Do you really think matches are a good idea? I mean, we're in the middle of a tree. Trees can burn." Juneth suggests in a whisper.

"Oh. But I can't see to go any further. I'll fall and these steps are too small," Alex answers "What should we do?" she asks.

As if on cue, the doorway that had magically opened starts closing and shutting out any chance for ambient light they did have.

Harmonia

The Sparkling Garden

The steps start collapsing and folding together to create a perfect tree trunk slide, sending the girls to their butts, and sliding faster than they have time to think to try to stop. Alex puts her hand down once but realizes that's a bad idea so she quickly pulls it back. Round and round they slide until. THUD!

A collected heap of Alex and Juneth lay tangled on the floor, as they try to collect their own separate appendage back to the original being, they hear the faint sound of music and see a glow down the narrow hallway. Thinking they must be at least 10 feet underground, Alex, looks around for any type of escape route. Nothing but walls of dirt and roots, and the smell of soil and worms. After first trying to climb back up the slide, like a school child, Alex decides they have no other alternative. They make their way cautiously toward the room with the music and easily push the door until the full room is in sight. And what a sight it is.

Harmonia

The Sparkling Garden

Chapter 9

Standing there, directly in front of them is such an odd creature, with tree roots for legs that resemble tentacles like an octopus, only they are made of tree bark. The five tentacle like roots, flick around, and move in unison to the giant, brown, trunk-like body. The face made out of knolls and knots has droopy eyes and bushy caterpillar like eyebrows. A small knot resembling a beauty mark rests below the lips at an area most likely resembling the chin of the tree face. An elongated knob for a nose, hangs between the droopy eyes, almost touching the lips. Giant bunches of shrubs gather at the top of the trunk, creating big poofs of hair-like bunches. The creature's long, branch-like fingers stretch out on both sides of its trunk body.

"I've been expecting you for some time," She speaks in a slow, drawn out, whispery old breath. She never bothers to look up as she moves around the room, giving what looks like medicine to a creature on one of the few tables.

The creature is small, and somewhat resembles a dragon, only, it's made out of tree roots. It has a long neck and a jagged snout that leans back to pointy, wooden ears. A highbrow of dirt and moss gather above the eyes, giving it the appearance of being angry. Yet, its eyes tell a story of being young and curious as it looks around the room. It coughs and a puff of smoke escapes its lips. It coo's and growls simultaneously.

Harmonia

"What is that?" whispers Alex leaning over to Juneth, who simply replies "Dracaena," as if it's common knowledge. Alex makes a mental note to ask about Dracaena later, and she glances around the room.

Around the compact and dark room there are a few metal tables, nooks resembling shelves, and cages with all kinds of strange hanging vines and mosses of greens and browns. There are jars and bowls full of different looking substances that look like organs, or other types or organisms. Upon reading some of the handwritten labels, it appears the gross things in the jars are used for cooking, healing, and some are just labeled miscellaneous. The room is dimly lit by only jars of the glowing rock they encountered earlier, and some carefully placed lightning bugs. A few electrically charged limbs from the tree itself lay around creating a little extra lighting as well.

"You must be the tree of wisdom?" Asks Alex, studying the busy bustling old tree. She gracefully bows as a sign of respect.

"No. You're inside the tree of wisdom. Name's Lora. I mend to the tree. Guess I can read the tree. It tells me things, and I tell it to you." She interrupts quickly, not once turning to look at the girls. "I'm told you come looking for the book."

"Yes ma'am. Can you help me find it?" Alex asks now feeling a little disrespected.

"No, but the tree can." Says Lora, frankly. And that's all she says as she goes back to mixing some kind soup or mush in the corner of the room. Only turning around once in a while to grab something off a shelf. A few moments of her bustling around goes by while Alex looks at Juneth and Juneth looks back at Alex with puzzled expressions.

"Well how can the tree talk to me then?" Alex finally pipes up, as she takes several steps closer to Lora.

Harmonia

At that, Lora turns and hands Alex the wooden pewter which she had been smashing all of the substances in just moments ago. The fluid inside smells like a rotten banana, looks like a squished up toad, and has the consistency of a thick jam. The pewter itself looks like an old rotting makeshift bowl.

"Drink this," says Lora, tipping the cup up to Alex's mouth before she has a chance to resist. Alex opens her mouth to object as the substance falls in a big plop in her mouth. She gags as she tries to swallow the substance that tastes like burnt plastic. It numbs her throat as it slides down, and she can feel it go all the way to her belly where she feels like a fire just started. She doubles over in pain and falls to her knees, feeling like she is going to be sick. Juneth runs over as Lora just goes back to mixing on the counter. Her ears start ringing and all sound fades out. She can see Juneth calling her but she can no longer hear her voice. Her eyes feel heavy.

That same old mirror is there, but this time the fog is lifted. In the reflection she can see her mother in a summer dress out in the yard at their old house. She looks like she's hanging laundry on the line. Alex looks over her shoulder, finding nothing but darkness, then back to the mirror where she watches her mother. She touches the glass, and her hand slides right on through. Her fingers pass through the surface of the mirror and she continues going through until she emerges in the yard with her mother.

She can smell the sweet musk of the perfume her mother used to wear, as she stands just observing and watching unbelievably. The flowers dance in the spring wind, as it wafts the perfume into the air, she closes her eyes remembering. Her mother works her way from one end to another hanging clothes, one by one, humming an old familiar song they used to sing. Alex can't remember the words exactly but knows it was about how her mother would always love her

Harmonia

and be there for her. At least that's what she thought it was about when she was younger.

"Unfortunately, I am not your mother, Alex," the woman speaks interrupting her nostalgia. "This is the only way I can speak to you in which you could understand. A language barrier, if you must."

Alex blinks and tries to process what she is saying. How can this not be her? She looks and sounds just like her. She is moving and humming about the yard, the same way she can remember her mother moving.

"But, this is how I remember you. Err, her," Alex says, very disappointed. "If you're not my mother than who are you, and why are you stealing my memories?" She asks, angrily balling her fists, and thinking this must be a trick of the void again, or a pixie.

"I'm the tree of wisdom. I am not stealing your memories, I'm just borrowing them so you can understand me. Did you understand me when I kept trying to grab your attention outside the trunk?" The tree asks, smiling.

"You mean the branches, when you were shocking me?" Alex asks remembering the jolt.

"Those were my words. You couldn't understand me, so I had to find a way to communicate. All plants try to communicate by releasing chemicals and making small movements. Like I said, it's a language barrier," she says now turning to look Alex in the face.

Alex is caught off guard by the real look of her mother's face. By her smell and the sound of her voice. By all the ways she moves and the way her hair blows in the breeze. She can't help feeling a heavy pain in her chest. It's been years since she's seen her mother's face and it sends a wave of remorse over her so heavy she actually flinches.

Harmonia

"Can you please be someone else? It hurts too badly for you to be her, and to know that she's not really real," Alex begs starting to cry.

"Everyone you know is only temporary, Alex, but the memory lives inside of you. It's not the memory that hurts, but knowing that the moment isn't any more than a memory. Because memories are only glimpses of small moments in our lives that are important. It's the meaning the memory had, in the first place, that makes it stick around. Think about this, you could go and recreate the moment all over again, but instead of having the same memory of it, you would have a different perspective, or a different point of view, because of what you know now. If I were to change to a different memory, it would affect you the same, because most memories are based on a deep love or a deep fear." The tree says, elegantly.

"But I miss her so much," Alex says falling down in tears. Her body heaving with huge sobs. The tree of wisdom comes over and starts stroking Alex's back lovingly, just the way her mother used to do.

After a moment Alex sits up and wipes her face, "but I don't understand," she starts in between sobs as she is frantically trying to clear her face, "out of all my memories, why would you pick this one?"

"Because it had to get your attention, and open you up to listen to me without being frightened or alarmed." The tree of wisdom says. "I know it's hard to do, but learning to rejoice in your memories, even the ones that make you sad, is the best way to keep them alive and happy."

"Ok." Says Alex in a small voice, feeling, once again, like the young broken girl she was that night her family was ripped away from her.

Harmonia

"Alex, we have to get to work, now, we don't have much time left." The tree of wisdom says, while pulling Alex to her feet and leading her over to the laundry she has piled in the basket on the ground. The basket has a crazy folded map in the shape of a cube, only the roads and places are 3d, like a popup book when it's unfolded. Alex looks closer and she can actually see Juneth, and Lora and the tree room and her own body, as she picks it up and unfolds it.

"This map is special. Keep it with you wherever you go. It changes depending on where you are and where you are heading." The Tree of Wisdom advises as she folds the map into a small cube and tucks it into Alex's hand. "Also here is a key, this will open many doors, but you must save it until you find the last door. You have one chance to use it Alex, after that it will disappear."

She hands Alex a heavy, long skeleton key on a rope that is cool on her chest as she puts it around her neck. The key is longer than her hand and each notch looks like a giant building the way it jets up and back down all jagged and each very different. The tarnished copper key is old and worn and you can barely make out some of the etchings that are covered in green.

"Last, but not least, I have the book," Informs the tree of wisdom quietly, but just as Alex starts to get excited and feel like this trip was finally coming to a close, The tree of wisdom says, "but most of the pages about the void have been ripped and scattered all over Harmonia and the surrounding worlds by Odium. I've put a protection around the one's I could find by hiding them with the last of my magic, but it's up to you now. Only the map can tell you the way. Beware Odium, he is the one behind the void. He is the darkness, and Alex he has seen your soul and your power, and he wants it for his own. He is after you now."

"I don't have any power!" Alex exclaims wildly. "I am a nobody!"

Harmonia

The Sparkling Garden

Chapter 10

"Alex you're going back now. The first page can be found in the Sinking Suds." She says hurriedly as Alex can feel herself being pulled back through the mirror sliding backward as the tree speaks. "And Alex," she hollers through cupped hands "Trust the unicorns."

"What do you mean?" she calls, but with that, Alex is back in the tree room with Juneth leaning over her and Lora back to attending to the dragon thing.

"See told you she'd be back," Lora says with an indifferent tone, while moving to another ledge to grab some more ingredients. This time she picks up a small flask made out of some type of ribbed animal skin. "Drink this. It'll help," she says shoving it in Alex's hands. Then noticing Alex's hesitation she says, "well go on, it's only a little drink to perk ya' back up from talking to 'er."

Alex turns it up a little, then a little more. It tastes like hot cinnamon, but with a cool refreshing aftertaste. Alex turns up the whole thing and gulp after gulp finishes it off. A small drop of fluid trickles out of the corner of her mouth and she quickly swipes it away and exhales really big. She didn't realize how thirsty she had become. Juneth slumps back in relief that Alex is back to consciousness.

"Seriously Alex, if you don't stop passing out my stalk is going to wither away from stress." Juneth says in a whispering faint voice.

Harmonia

"Where did you go? What happened?" she asks curiously, now sitting back upright and moving closer so she can hear everything.

"I met the tree of wisdom, and she gave me this map," Alex says pulling the cube out of her pocket and lying it on the floor where it opens and shows them and the entire room. "She said the void was created by Odium. And that he's after me. And….THE BOOK! I forgot the book." Alex starts looking around frantically. "Lora, I need to go back, I left the book."

"Child, the tree has the book. You can't go back, only forward." Lora says cryptically as she goes back to attending her sick animals.

"So if the tree has the book, then it could be here?" Alex asks after a few moments, but Lora just looks slyly at her. "But where?"

Alex and Juneth start looking around at all the shelves and under things and under tables. Lora seems annoyed but just goes about her business as if nothing is going on. She keeps glancing at them every so often and shaking her head.

"You got a map." Lora says, finally, after watching them knock on walls and keep searching.

"But how is that going to tell me where the book is?" Alex asks as Juneth sits down and starts studying it closely.

"Alex, come look!" Juneth calls excitedly "there's something weird on the top of the tree! I think it's a book!" Alex comes running over to where Juneth is in the floor. There it is. A glowing speck at the very top of the tree, glowing on the map.

"Ok, but how do we get on top of the tree?" asks Alex. Both girls sit there and think a few minutes.

Harmonia

"Maybe I could climb it?" Alex suggests with a hopeful look on her face.

"Yeah remember how holding the branch went?" Juneth recalls Alex being electrocuted multiple times by the tree, with a look of disapproval.

"Oh yeah. Let's not try that again. Well, is there a ladder?" Alex suggests looking at Lora, who pays them no mind and just continues picking ingredients and smashing more into the pewter, and humming.

They shrug their shoulders and go back to brainstorming. Making suggestion after suggestion, one crazier than the last. Alex even suggests catching enough butterflies and tying strings around them until they lift her or Juneth up to the book. But there is the problem with coming down that they haven't quite figured out.

Lora turns and pours the pink liquid mixture into a small plastic test tube and hands it to Alex.

"Drink that when you get outside. It'll take you how high you need to go. But be careful, you'll come down pretty quick like." Lora explains in her disassociated way, and goes back to her business

Juneth and Alex look at the map one last time, then Alex picks it up as it folds into a small cube again and she places it in her bag. They thank Lora, who pretends not to hear them, and head for the door from which they first entered. The spiral slide has now become steps again and the staircase is as dark as a deep cave. They slowly and steadily make their way to the top one step at a time.

Shielding their eyes from the sunshine, they make their way in between the droopy branches and on the outskirts of the tree. Alex hands Juneth her bag, and takes one long gulp from the test tube liquid. Nothing happens.

Harmonia

"Umm. Maybe I should jump?" Alex asks.

"With Lora, It's hard to tell. She doesn't explain things well," Juneth admits "I mean quite frankly, I'm surprised you didn't pass out again," Juneth jests, and Alex starts laughing.

Just then, Alex starts lifting slowly off the ground. "Wait! I don't know how to steer." Alex yells flapping her arms.

"Try leaning your body a little toward the tree." Juneth suggests. Alex leans forward and then she flips all the way over, and over, and over again. Finally getting back to a steady point she maneuvers upright again, accidentally contacting one of the branches and jumping at the jolt.

"Maybe not that much." Juneth calls laughing, "try just a little bit."

Alex leans very carefully this time as her body is still slowly climbing and she starts to head for the middle of the tree. She leans just a little bit more and swoops the book up as she continues to climb. The book is big and heavier in her hands than she expected it to be. It almost topples her into a spin again.

"Ok. I got the book, but how do I get down?" Alex calls starting to wonder if she'll float all the way up into the sky.

"Ummm, that, I have no idea." Juneth calls back, somewhat troubled, looking around for a solution.

Alex slowly stops rising so high. She can see everything from here. The bug city, the big forest and way off in the distance she can see the mountain. She looks down to tell Juneth what she sees but Juneth looks just like a tiny little dot. A little to Juneth's left and there's a small glimpse of a sparkle hiding just under a ledge under a tree.

Harmonia

The Sparkling Garden

Just as Alex turns her focus on that sparkle, she starts dropping out of the sky at an alarming rate. She almost drops the book in surprise, but is able to catch it at the last minute. Still the quick falling has her worried about the drop at the end. She starts fanning her arm and leaning this way and that way, to try to slow herself down, with no luck.

"Please, please don't drop me," she says out loud to gravity.

Down below, Juneth notices Alex's speedy descent and runs around frantic trying to find something for her to land on. Picking up piles of leaves and anything else even remotely soft that might cushion her fall. Alex starts grasping at anything in the air as her hands land on the tree's branches, which shock and electrocute her with every brush, so she lets go quickly.

She starts slowing down just as her feet are about to impact the ground and she shuts her eyelids as tight as a mason jar. Her feet softly kiss the ground and slowly she feels all of her weight come back. Juneth falls over with a huge sigh of relief.

"Honestly Alex, you're going to be the death of me!" She exclaims, running to hug Alex as they both giggle. "What does it look like? What does it say?" Juneth asks excitedly reaching to touch the book.

The giant book is as big as Alex's lap and the cover is heavy velvet with metallic clasps. The book itself is brown and tarnished. Like the doors in Harmonia, the book's cover has animated carvings that move. Some are flowers, others are vines, like the ones navigated by Juneth and Alex earlier that day. The book is thick and has that old library smell to it. Alex pulls open the front cover and as if by magic, a scrawl of small cursive words start appearing in gold lettering. Alex starts flipping through the pages slowly; finding stories about the

Harmonia

The Sparkling Garden

unicorns, and how Harmonia came to be, some are just memories of
silly things that happened. Finally, they get to the pages about Odium.

Harmonia

The Sparkling Garden

Chapter 11

The book tells about how Odium lived among all the beings in the beginning. He lived during the time of unicorns and was a noble in that age. It was just after the Universe had created Harmonia. He was always very curious about magic and harvesting magic, but he did so in the name of science, with good intention and never hurting anyone. He was an explorer and world renown for finding ancient truths. It is said that Odium, one day, stumbled upon some ancient buried magic in one of the realms and came back maniacal.

He started talking about harvesting the unicorns and using their horns for greatness beyond words. It's said that he initiated the war between beings and unicorns, causing them to go into hiding. When the unicorns went into hiding, Odium went on an expedition to find them taking only a small crew of supporters and some of the magic he had acquired. The entire crew became lost and no one had heard from, or about Odium since that day. People had assumed that he too, had been unfortunately departed due to his greed.

Years went by, and most beings forgot about the incident all together. Those who did remember, only remembered in bits and pieces. And as stories were retold, the more unbelievable they became, to the point where beings only used them for fun, and to teach lessons. Some stories went as far as turning him into a horrendous, monstrosity of a being.

Harmonia

The Sparkling Garden

The following section on the void only has a small snippet of information, the rest of the pages have been torn out. It says:

The void is a tear in the existence of time and space, and can only be created through powerful magic and many sacrifices of legendary power. The first instance of the void was reported back in the beginning time of the unicorns, but it was repaired right away due to the overwhelming magic of all the unicorns in existence at that time. Since then there have been no other instances known.

That's where the page is torn. That's all the information on the void. Alex thumbs through a few more pages, finding stories on the sparkling gardens and some about pixies, but nothing about how to stop the void.

"Wow! Maybe you were right about the unicorns," Juneth says apologetically to Alex.

"Ha! I told you," shouts Alex smiling gleefully, from ear to ear.

"So that could also mean that you made the rain!" Says Juneth smirking like a child who just ate the last piece of chocolate cake.

"Ugg! Juneth! For the last time, that was a strange coincidence. I did not make the rain." Alex grumbles.

"Well, we better take this back to Thomas, in Harmonia. He and Seb can look at it, and we can all decide where we should start." Juneth suggests, as she starts to make her way back toward the Ravine.

"Wait," says Alex suddenly, "I remember seeing something sparkle over in the grass when I was floating in the sky." She points and starts running to the ledge, where she had found the sparkling spot. Juneth stands there watching Alex search around, looking at her with curiosity.

Harmonia

The Sparkling Garden

"Alex, this is the Sparkling Garden, things tend to sparkle a lot here. It's probably a beetle or just a flower" Juneth advises shrugging her shoulders and slowly walking away.

Alex keeps searching determinedly, knowing she saw something. She notices a tiny glisten on a large rock, so she reaches down to pick it up. The rock won't come out of the ground, so she gives it a slight twist to wiggle it free, and the ground starts shaking. Part of the ledge starts shifting to reveal a small tunnel. Alex looks over to Juneth with a look of satisfaction. Juneth stands there looking terrified, then starts making her way over to the cave.

"But you don't know where that leads." Juneth says objectively, "and what if there are more chasms?" Juneth mentions shivering and looking around anxiously.

"You're right. Let's look on the map." Alex suggests pulling it out of her bag and setting it open on the ground. "Besides, going back the way we came, means we'll definitely face chasms. At least we can see if this is another way. Maybe we can avoid them," she suggests trying to get Juneth on board with the plan.

The map shows the tunnel before them, but it doesn't show where the tunnel leads. It only shows the entrance to the tunnel. The girls twist the map and try to turn it but each time it only shows the entrance and darkness. Like an emptiness etched into the center of the map.

"Maybe we have to go inside. If we open the map inside the tunnel, it might tell us where to go?" Alex suggests, because frankly, she has no other explanation as to why the map isn't working.

Alex picks up the map and it folds back into its tiny cube shape, then the girls slowly tuck their way inside the dark cave. They see a light in the distance, so they inch forward, slowly closing the gap between them and the light ahead. After what seems like forever,

Harmonia

they come into this room that has foreign patterns that glows eerily all over the rock and dirt. There are rocks formed into a circle in the center, and weird markings scrawled into the floor. Ambient glowing comes from a few lights around the area. A few desk like objects litter the room, and a table with more weird marks. Juneth grabs Alex's hand and pulls her back just in time to save her from stepping into the middle of the weird circle.

"We are not supposed to be here." Juneth whispers trying to pull Alex back.

"What do you mean, Juneth?" Alex asks still curiously snooping around "What is all of this stuff?"

"Dark magic," Juneth whispers tugging at Alex, trying to get her to go back from where they came from.

Just then, they hear a bustling, moving, sound coming from the far side of the cave, so they each crouch under a separate desk, where they notice rocks in the wall start opening up like a weird puzzle. A giant being made of black, ashen rock emerges. A bulbous figure that looks like he has tar running down his stone body. He stands about 7 feet tall and is as wide as a tank. He resembles a large bulky boulder that burst out of a hot volcano. The creature has large red spines protruding from his torso jetting out in all different places. The spikes are made more prominent as he turns carrying a decaying deer body toward the center of the circle. He marches like he has some authority. He looks up with dark eyes that seem to be made of onyx, as he places the deer in the floor, and starts chanting in some old language. His voice booming like a thunderbolt, but peculiarly empty and monotone.

The deer body seems to seep into the lines of the circle and slowly dissipates as the beings' chants grow louder and louder. The circle begins to glow, and a deep purple light rises up from each line,

Harmonia

creating a purple haze around the chanting being. The haze starts a slow swirl around the cave as it darkens from purple to gray. Alex recognizes this haze, as the one from her dream. The sulfuric burning smell fills the air and she stifles a cough, as the swirling fog begins to lift, quickly spiraling toward the ceiling of the cave, exposing an empty cave. The creature seems to have vanished like that of a magician's smoke screen.

As the fog clears, Juneth and Alex slowly emerge. Alex, teary eyed, finally coughs and catches her breath. They carefully creep toward the door that they entered through, and emerge back in the Sparkling Garden before either of the girls gather the courage to speak.

"What just happened?" Alex asks unbelievably, voice still a bit raspy from the fog.

"I'm not really sure," admits Juneth, "but we better get back to Thomas and tell him everything we know. He'll know how to handle what is going on." She offers assuredly as they hurriedly rush out of the cave. They shield their eyes from the sun upon emerging and take off walking briskly away from the secret cave that closes back when they exit. Lora emerges from under the Weeping Willow's branches shouting something inaudible, but she's waving for them to come back.

"I wonder what she wants?" asks Juneth almost to herself.

"I'm not sure, but this is the most animated we've seen Lora, so we better go see what it is. It might be important," Alex retorts thoughtfully. The girls start walking back up the embankment toward the Tree of Wisdom.

"I forgot something very important," Lora persists once the girls get within ear-shot, "you must come see."

Harmonia

"What is it?" They ask panting as they make their way to her a little quicker.

Juneth and Alex trek their way back up the hill and without a word further, Lora leads them once again under the electric filled branches, and into the hole in the tree, down the steps that turn into a slide, and back to the underground tree room. The girls stop and look baffled as Lora goes right back over to the shelves and starts pulling at things and moving things around, mumbling incoherently under her breath.

"Lora," Alex starts, careful not to approach her again for fear of being forced to drink another odd tonic, "what is this all about?"

Lora pulls out an old rusty handle of some sort and holds it out for Alex to grab from her. "Here it is. I almost forgot." She says as she flicks it in her hand a moment, beckoning for Alex to approach.

"Oh. Umm. Gee. Thank you Lora." Alex quips trying to sound grateful, while unbelievably turning over the handle in her hand squinting and studying it. It's a brown and rusty looking round knob that attaches to just a flat base. It is very bulky and overall heavy. Alex's first thought is to throw it down, as soon as they get back outside. It is very much like Lora to make them trek all this way for a rusty old knob.

"Well go on. Back to Harmonia with yuns." Lora nudges feeling mighty proud of herself, smiling from ear to ear.

Juneth and Alex begin to head for the stairs once again when Lora stops them again.

"Aren't you going to use it?" She asks candidly.

"Use what?" Alex asks looking at Lora, very confused.

Harmonia

"Well the Harmonious Handle of course," Lora banters back affirmatively, as if the audacity to even ask was such a wild notion.

"I don't. Umm. Know exactly what you're referring," Alex stammers confused, "Do you mean this old, rusty thing?" she asks holding up the doorknob.

"Well, give it here," Lora reaches back over and yanks the knob out of Alex's hand, "I'm only showing you this one time. Pay attention."

She takes the knob over to the wall at the furthest side of the room. The wall that isn't all covered in shelves, and she holds the handle perpendicular to the wall and knocks three times with the other hand. She then twists the handle counterclockwise four spins and clockwise two. Like magic, the wall becomes a door before their very eyes and she opens the door, and the elegance of the great hallway of Harmonia greets them.

Harmonia

The Sparkling Garden

Chapter 12

"Whoa!" The girls both exclaim at once. Very excited to see Harmonia so close to their fingertips.

"Once you have the door open, you can slide the knob off the side of the door, but be quick. Once the handle is removed you only have a few moments before the doorway closes." Lora explains quickly, sliding the knob toward the open side of the door and thrusting the handle in Alex's hand as the girls make their way through the small doorway. "And always remember to get the handle before…" Lora shouts as the door slowly closes and her voice is shut out, leaving the girls back in Harmonia. Alex stores the knob in her bag once again before looking around the hallway.

The silence of the hallway almost pierces Juneth and Alex's ears, as they quietly take in their surroundings for a few moments. It seems like decades ago, they first began this journey, and now being back feels almost too good to be true. Alex is already fantasizing about the comfy cloud bed and wonderful warm meal, and Juneth pictures Frank's creepy face. A smile approaches both of their faces before they look at each other, and take off running toward the banquet room.

The girls swing open the door, and there sits Frank at one side of the table, pretty much nodding off, with his head bobbing backward

Harmonia

and his body slumped lazily in the chair. Seb sits there, straight as an arrow, tapping away at a calculator. Thomas sits at the end, with a leg thrown over the arm of his chair, thoughtfully spinning a pencil while staring at the ceiling.

As they hear the door swing open they turn to see the girls standing in the doorway. Juneth looking pitifully bare, still without many leaves, and Alex covered in dirt, mud, slime, and every other disgusting thing they encountered. Thomas leaps up immediately and dashes toward them. Seb stops tapping on his calculator and almost seems to smile. And Frank, jumps awake, wipes the sleep from his eye, which turns into a green gooey glob that he quickly wipes on the underside of the table. He smiles a huge boney grin as one side of his jaw detaches and hangs awkwardly swinging as he stands and rushes to hug Juneth.

Thomas swoops up Alex, and spins her around. "You're back! I knew you could do it, do you have the book?" He asks excitedly then he waves his hand, "Oh never mind! Just welcome back! Tell us about your journey. Are you hungry? Of course you're hungry. C'mon. Sit." He gestures still exhilarated, as Seb gets up from the table and goes into the kitchen to retrieve some plates of food. Alex feels dizzy from the excitement and plops into the chair Thomas has pulled out for her.

Within moments Seb begins ushering in warm, steaming plates of delicious looking food that smells like a breakfast feast. Frank has stopped hugging Juneth, who is as red as a fire truck, and he pulls out a chair for her as she bashfully bats her eyelashes and giggles anxiously.

Without words Juneth and Alex dig into the food, like two ravenous cavemen that have been hibernating for a month without food. You can almost hear growls come from their mouths as they demolish every morsel in front of their faces. When they look up and see Thomas, Frank and Seb staring wildly with smirks on their faces,

Harmonia

almost looking scared, the girls pull back and start eating a bit more daintily but still hurriedly.

Finally, with full bellies, the girls sit back and start talking about their adventure, starting from the beginning. Sometimes excitedly talking over each other and trying to include every detail. They both shiver when they talk about the chasms and start trying to describe them. Haunting memories flood their minds, as they try to physically shake the images from their heads.

"You were right to suggest not trusting the pixies," admits Alex. "I just wish I would have known what a pixie was before it bit me." They all start laughing as Alex describes how intrigued she was by the tiny pixie. They all gather up on elbows and alike to hear about the void and the creepy tree. Alex leaves out the part about the unicorns, not wanting to have the "hallucination" debate again.

When they reach the part of the story about the bees, and the sudden burst of rain, Juneth insists that Alex made the rain, which catches added attention from Thomas, who sits up straighter, and looks very intently at her, almost making her feel uncomfortable.

"I didn't make the rain," Alex insists again "That's absurd," appalled that he would even give her a questioning look about something so crazy.

"Is it?" Thomas asks as she breaks his gaze and looks away. Her mind starts to wander back to those memories with her mother. Juneth carries on with the story of their adventure. It all happened very strangely with the bees, and the rain, right when she thought it. Why is Thomas staring at her so intently? Does he know something? She looks up and tries to pay attention to Juneth recapping their adventure, with a smile on her face, but her mind is so many places. What does it all mean?

Harmonia

"Well, you girls look tired," Thomas says catching Alex's distant look, "We should all rest, and discuss the book in length when we are feeling more alert." He winks at Alex as she agrees quickly.

They all agree, say their goodnights, and head to their rooms. Alex glances over her shoulder, and sees Thomas watching her go into the cloud bedroom she first awoke in. What isn't he telling her, she wonders? He smiles coyly, and pivots, skipping toward the ocean door.

Harmonia

The Sparkling Garden

Chapter 13

After showering and getting comfortable, Alex lies down on the fluffy white bed and pulls the blankets up to her chin. Rolling on her side, a million thoughts are turning through her mind. She feels like she is at the stage of exhaustion where you can't even fall asleep. She tosses and turns from side to side. Thoughts of the book, and her "making the rain," flood her brain. There are so many questions. Will they ever be answered? Sleep finds her at last, moments before Seb enters the room to bring her breakfast.

Alex sits up tiredly and grinds the sleep from her eyes as she dreads the discussion about the book, and any more rain making talk that might come up. She nibbles on some of the food before combing her hair back into a loose pony tail, and entering the large hallway. She meanders down the hallway slowly and enters the dining room, apparently interrupting a private discussion. This is made evident by the immediate silence upon her entry, and the guilty look on Juneth's face.

"I swear, if you guys are talking about the rain again," Alex begins as she sits down rubbing her head.

"Do you feel ok, Alex?" Thomas asks as he gets up and pours Alex some of the sweet nectar drink.

Harmonia

The Sparkling Garden

"I didn't sleep well," she says coldly as she takes a sip of the drink and sets the cup back down. "So, what were we talking about?" She asks.

"What does the book say about the void?" Thomas deflects, successfully trying to start another topic.

"There isn't much information. Most of the pages have been torn and scattered among Harmonia," Alex informs, feeling a bit sorry for her irrational reaction to interrupting their conversation. "The only pages we have tell us that Odium created the first occurrence of the void and the unicorns repaired the only existence of the void earlier to this one. The tree of wisdom said she knows definitely of one of the pages in the Sinking Suds?"

"Unicorns? But I thought those were just stories?" Thomas asks incredulously, smiling like a little boy, more amused with the thought of a unicorn, than finding the next page.

"Seriously?" Alex asks, obviously annoyed. "You guys can live on clouds, and think that a person made the rain, but you don't believe in unicorns?" Alex then starts chuckling and crying at the same time. She realizes she looks crazy, but after everything she just went through and everything she has learned, she does not care how she looks anymore.

Thomas walks over to her and rubs her back trying to console her. He motions for the others to leave and give them a moment, as they quietly get out of their chairs and move toward the door, they look back sadly at Alex. Thomas talks softly to Alex as she sobs loudly.

"Alex, we know you're scared and that this is a lot to take in," he says consolingly. "You don't have to do this alone. We are all with you. We are all here to help."

Harmonia

"Help? How are you guys helping? You are the ones making me think I'm crazy. Talking about making the rain, and finding lost books, and seeing unicorns..." Alex continues ranting.

"You saw a unicorn?" Thomas interrupts happily.

"Yes, twice!" she stops and looks into Thomas's eyes, trying to figure out if he's just humoring her then decides to go on "I told Juneth but she didn't believe me."

"When did you see the unicorn? Before you made the rain?" Thomas asks excitedly and then immediately wishes he could take back the last question. "I mean, ummm..."

"Thomas, I did not make the rain. Even if it were possible, I don't know the first thing about magic, or making weather," Alex insists, pounding her fist against the table, pleading with Thomas to understand.

"Alex, come with me," Thomas insists. They get up and walk out into the hallway, and walk toward the oceanic room that Alex had first met Thomas after coming to Harmonia. They walk through the giant bellowing door and step into the ocean floor again, walking past fish and whales alike, sand squishing with every step. A giant shark swims past, not giving one notice to Alex's increased heart rate at the sight. They walk in silence for miles until the water starts getting shallower and they slowly start to emerge onto a white beach. There is nothing but sands and ocean for miles around this tiny little piece of land. The land itself has a small patch of palm trees that gently sway.

Thomas, stops, not saying a word and just looks at Alex, with a deep intent. He looks back over the ocean and out toward the skies. He looks out past the horizon where a patch of gray clouds lay, never saying a word about where they are.

Harmonia

"Do you think, it wasn't scary for me, or Seb, or Juneth?" He asks after a long moment of awkward silence. "We knew from birth that these halls and worlds were our responsibilities, and it was still hard for us. We had to work and develop powers that we needed, sometimes feeling like failures, trying to make our magic work for us. You have a power, Alex. Whether you want to believe it or not, your power is greater than all of ours together. What we have worked hard to achieve, was just given to you from birth. We thought giving you the chance to achieve it on your own, would prove to you who you are to us, but you're still fighting it. You're still fighting us, and we need you!"

"Thomas, I don't know how or where to start," Alex starts sadly, having a new understanding of why they have persisted so hard for Alex.

"You start by taking responsibility, and by believing in yourself," Thomas says, boldly. "Our lives rest in your abilities."

"What if I can't do it?" Alex asks, tears gliding down her cheeks, then pausing just for a moment before dripping off her chin to disappear in the sand.

Thomas reaches up and turns her chin toward his face. "We know you can do it. I know you can," he says quietly looking into her eyes. Her heart flutters and she feels butterflies in her stomach.

She blushes and turns toward the ocean wishing she could feel a warm wind. An enormous gust even. She closes her eyes and pictures the clouds moving and the sun beaming down on her face with a warm gust of wind. At that very moment the clouds move and open the sun on her face as a strong wind picks up first just ruffling the leaves on the trees then blowing a sand storm right beside them as Alex lifts her arms. Thunder bellows from the clouds as if to say "Here I am!" Thomas stands there smiling in wonder at Alex and the

Harmonia

wind. She lets out a deep breath and lets down her arms knowing this is her power and this is where she belongs. She will do what is necessary to save Harmonia. The wind dies down and she opens her eyes to look at Thomas, who is smiling back at her as if to say, "I knew you had it in you." And for the first time in her life, she feels alive.

J.C Perez

www.ingramcontent.com/pod-product-compliance
Lightning Source LLC
Chambersburg PA
CBHW022047170626
46808CB00003B/1392